50 ¢

Binder removed his sports jacket and draped it across the back of his chair before he sat down. The storm outside had upped the humidity in the room. "In answer to your question, Mr. MacGillivray came in to provide Will Orsolini with an alibi. He says he saw Mr. Orsolini on the other side of Herrickson's Point at the relevant time."

That raised an interesting question. "What is the relevant time?"

"Between 11:05 AM and 11:34 AM," Flynn answered.

"That's precise."

"You gave us the 11:05 time," Binder reminded me.

"I was keeping track carefully that morning. I didn't want to miss the *Jacquie II*. How did you get the later time?"

"The call saying there was a body at Herrickson House came into 911 at 11:17 AM. Your friend Officer Dawes was first on the scene at 11:34 AM. Frick was dead when Officer Dawes found him."

"Who called 911?"

"Anonymous. From an extension inside the house."

Inside the house? That was creepy. "A man or a woman?" I asked.

"Man."

The hair on my arms stood up. "Do you think he was the killer? Because if he was, and he murdered Frick and called 911 twelve minutes after I left, that probably means—" I shuddered.

"He was already in the house when you were there . . .

Books by Barbara Ross

CLAMMED UP

BOILED OVER

MUSSELED OUT

FOGGED INN

ICED UNDER

STOWED AWAY

STEAMED OPEN

EGG NOG MURDER
(with Leslie Meier and Lee Hollis)

YULE LOG MURDER
(with Leslie Meier and Lee Hollis)

Published by Kensington Publishing Corporation

STEAMED OPEN

Barbara Ross

KENSINGTON BOOKS
www.kensingtonbooks.com

KENSINGTON BOOKS are published by

Kensington Publishing Corp.
119 West 40th Street
New York, NY 10018

All Kensington titles, imprints, and distributed lines are available at special quantity discounts for bulk purchases for sales promotion, premiums, fund-raising, educational, or institutional use.

Special book excerpts or customized printings can also be created to fit specific needs. For details, write or phone the office of the Kensington Sales Manager: Attn.: Sales Department. Kensington Publishing Corp., 119 West 40th Street, New York, NY 10018. Phone: 1-800-221-2647.

Kensington and the K logo Reg. U.S. Pat. & TM Off.

First Printing: January 2019
ISBN-13: 978-1-4967-1794-8
ISBN-10: 1-4967-1794-5

ISBN-13: 978-1-4967-1797-9 (ebook)
ISBN-10: 1-4967-1797-X (ebook)

10 9 8 7 6 5 4 3 2 1

Printed in the United States of America

This book is dedicated to my Wicked Cozy Authors: Jessie Crockett (Jessica Ellicott), Sherry Harris, Julie Hennrikus (Julia Henry), Edith Maxwell (Maddie Day), and Liz Mugavero (Cate Conte). You've been with me on every step of this adventure and I couldn't have done it without your laughter, love, and support.

CHAPTER 1

I glanced at my phone to catch the time. If our tour boat, the *Jacquie II*, didn't leave the town pier soon, we'd never be back in time to take the lunch customers to Morrow Island for our authentic Maine clambake.

Under normal circumstances, we never took the boat out before the first group of the day. But today we were fulfilling a mission we couldn't refuse. Three weeks earlier, immediately before Heloise (Lou) Herrickson had passed away at the age of a hundred and one, she'd given her housekeeper an exacting set of instructions written in her spidery cursive hand. One of them had been for her ashes to be consigned to the sea from the *Jacquie II*, because it was the only tour boat in the harbor large enough to hold all her friends.

And friends she had. As I searched through the colorful crowd (no one wearing black, as she'd instructed), I was astonished by how many of Busman's Harbor's citizens had taken a morning during August, the busiest month of the year, to say good-bye to Lou. We had on board, literally, a butcher, a baker, and three candlestick makers. (Every resort town has at least one candle shop.) Plus, hairdressers, manicurists, handymen, gardeners, artists, and enough wait staff, bartenders, and musicians to throw a ball. There were more than a hundred people.

My family was well represented by my mom, my sister, her husband, and me. My boyfriend Chris was there, too. It was a rare opportunity for us to be together during daylight hours in peak tourist season. On the coast of Maine, we had four short months to make our money and that meant Chris and I spent fifteen hours a day on the job, or in his case, jobs. I leaned back against him, my small body fitting perfectly against his rangy, muscular one. He put an arm around my shoulder and squeezed. He wasn't much for public displays of affection, so I treasured his reassurance. I was happy to be outside on a beautiful summer day, which was exactly what Lou would have wanted.

As I looked around the boat, I knew almost everyone. There were a few people I didn't—a couple in matching sweatshirts emblazoned with the silhouette of the Rockland Breakwater Lighthouse, and a woman in her seventies with leathery skin that bespoke years of tanning—but they were rare exceptions.

Everyone who should have been on the boat was there, happily chatting as we waited at the Busman's Harbor town pier. Everyone except Lou's grandnephew and heir. As the big engine of the

Jacquie II idled, passengers looked over toward the dock, waiting, waiting.

There was more than a little curiosity about Bartholomew Frick around town. Lou's home on Herrickson Point was a local landmark, a huge shingle-style pile overlooking a beach and her privately owned lighthouse. The land and buildings had been in Lou's late husband's family for generations. Everyone wanted to meet the man who was going to inherit.

Through the back window of the pilothouse, Captain George mouthed, "What's up?" I shrugged, the universal symbol for "dunno," then pointed to an imaginary watch on my wrist and held up five fingers. We'd wait five more minutes for Bartholomew Frick and then leave whether he was on board or not. Lou had been a wonderful, generous woman. How could her only heir be late for her final journey?

From the pier came the sound of a powerful motor and the sight of tourists scattering for cover. A red convertible Porsche squealed to a stop in front of the *Jacquie II*. A man in his mid-forties jumped out. He was medium-height, had a thick head of brown hair and wore khakis, a white tailored shirt, a blue blazer, no tie and no socks. I took all this in as he ran toward the boat.

I made my way through the crowd muttering "excuse me, excuse me," to the mourners as I passed. The man and I arrived at top of the gangway at the same moment.

"Mr. Frick? I'm sorry. You can't park there." He kept his head down so he could pretend not to see me and tried to dodge around me. I stepped into his path.

From behind me, Chris whispered, "You need help?"

I was grateful for the offer. "No, thanks. I've got this.

"Mr. Frick, I'm Julia Snowden. I own this boat." (A slight inaccuracy. My mother did, but I was in charge of this particular journey.) "You can't park on the town pier. The space you're in is for loading and unloading passengers only." He'd passed about a dozen signs telling him so as he'd made his way from Main Street to the pier.

He pulled his head up and looked me in the face for the first time. "I'm sorry. What did you say?"

I repeated myself, slowly and clearly.

"Where am I to put my car?" he demanded. "Every parking space in town is taken."

Ah, tourist season. The locals on the *Jacquie II* had known parking would be a problem. Many had walked, or arrived in plenty of time to find a space. Others had even (shudder) parked in one of the paid lots, regarded as the ultimate sacrifice. They'd done it because they loved Lou Herrickson.

I could have directed her grandnephew to one of those paid lots, but the nearest one was blocks away and there was no guarantee it would have any spots left open. So instead, I said, "You can park in my mother's driveway. It's just up the street. Forty-three Main."

He grunted, then hesitated. I thought he might

argue and at that point I would have let him leave the car on the pier where it would certainly be towed. Finally, he acquiesced. "Wait for me."

I told him we'd wait five minutes.

I turned and saw Chris. He'd taken a few steps back and stood with arms crossed over his chest, in his bouncer pose, making sure everything was okay. I smiled at him and then went to tell Captain George the new plan. He fussed and fumed about being late to pick up the first shift of clambake guests who would be waiting when we got back. "You can do it," I encouraged him. "For Lou."

"For Lou," he repeated. I knew there were few people, living or dead, for whom he would have agreed.

To his credit, Frick did keep a move on. He came pelting up the gangway with seconds to spare. As he jumped onto the boat, Captain George called to the kids who worked the lines. They let us loose and we powered away from the pier.

We pulled back to the pier an hour and fifteen minutes later. As Captain George had predicted, there was already a long line of smiling, excited tourists with tickets for the luncheon seating at the Snowden Family Clambake. The mourners filed off the *Jacquie II* quickly. It had been a rare social occasion for them, one full of laughter and a few tears as friends had taken turns reminiscing about their encounters with the indomitable Heloise Herrickson, but they had businesses to attend to.

Bartholomew Frick rushed off with the rest of

them, not acknowledging the other guests, his great-aunt's friends and neighbors. During the memorial, Frick had been tight-lipped, declining to speak about his great-aunt, or even to take a handful of her ashes to cast into the sea.

I didn't have time to wonder about his behavior as he hurried off the pier. I had my hands full. My sister Livvie and her husband Sonny left the *Jacquie II* and jumped into our Boston Whaler, which was also tied up at the pier. Sonny was our bake master, overseeing the tower of hot rocks that cooked the lobsters, clams, corn, onions, potatoes, and eggs we served to the guests. Livvie ran the kitchen that put out the clam chowder along with the blueberry grunt we served for dessert.

I gave my sister a hug as she ran by. "It was good of you to come," I said. It had taken meticulous planning to have our employees cover both the clambake fire and the kitchen, as well as care for my ten-year-old niece and six-month-old nephew. Fortunately, it was the best time of year for it. By mid-August the clambake team was experienced, running at its peak, and we hadn't yet started losing the college students and out-of-state teachers whose jobs seemed to start earlier every year.

Chris lingered until all the mourners were off the boat and before the lunch customers boarded. Given his feelings about public displays of affection, he surprised me by giving me a quick kiss and whispering, "I love you," in my ear.

I kissed him back. "Love you, too. See you tonight."

"I'll be late," he said.

"I know."

Once the lunch guests were on board, we pulled back into the harbor. Captain George narrated the tour. As we passed the harbor islands, he pointed out the seals sunning themselves, the bald eagle perched in an evergreen, and the osprey's nest on the rocky outcropping beside Dinkum's Light. Only someone who'd been on the trip as often as I had would have noticed that he'd shortened it by ten minutes or so, making up the time lost to the memorial.

As the *Jacquie II* left the warm embrace of Busman's Harbor and entered the Gulf of Maine, guests shrugged into sweatshirts or windbreakers. I offered blankets to those who, back when they were in the August heat on the mainland, hadn't read or believed our advice to bring something warm to wear on the water.

Ten minutes later, just as the little ones on board were getting antsy, Morrow Island appeared ahead. As we drew closer to the long dock, the features of the island came into focus, the little house where Livvie and Sonny and their kids lived in the summer on one side of the dock, and the clambake fire on a long, flat expanse on the other. On the island's first plateau was the dining pavilion that housed about half our tables, plus the gift shop, bar, and our tiny kitchen. Along the flat green space once called the great lawn were the volleyball nets and bocce courts for the guests. At the highest point on the island was the partially burned ruin of my ancestors' mansion, Windsholme. A year after the fire, plans to restore it were underway. But our guests couldn't see that.

All they could see were the boarded up windows and roof, and the ugly orange hazard fence that surrounded her.

I moved to starboard to help the crew tie the lines and to be the first one on the dock in order to greet our guests. They came off the boat, taking in the rugged island and the smells of salt water, evergreens, and wood smoke. Le Roi, the island's Maine coon cat, ran to greet them. Maine coons have many doglike qualities, greeting people being only one, but in Le Roi's case I suspected a larger agenda. If he charmed our patrons now, they'd be more apt to slip him a piece of lobster or a clam as he lingered under their tables.

The guests spread out, some to the bar, some to play games, some to find the perfect table, perhaps in a grove overlooking the ocean. The more ambitious hiked up to Windsholme or all the way to the beach on the other side of the island. I watched them go, but only for a second, and then ran up the walk to the dining pavilion. Showtime!

The height of the season and the late start for the boat combined to create a busy lunch seating. I moved among the guests, showing this one how to use the crackers to open the lobster's claws, and that one how to dredge the steamers in the clam juice before eating them. I was tired by the time we waved the customers off at the dock and happy to sit down to our family meal while the *Jacquie II* returned to the harbor and picked up the next group.

Family meal was my favorite part of the day. In the quiet time between the lunch and dinner rushes, all our employees sat down together to enjoy our own food. Livvie and her crew in the kitchen whipped up something inexpensive and hearty to fill up people who had done the tough, physical work to ensure that our customers had a marvelous time. Often, we took advantage of our pipeline to fresh, local seafood. Today, the cooks presented us with linguini with clam sauce and an enormous summer salad. The food and cold drinks were on the bar, buffet style. The clam sauce smelled briny and fresh, like the ocean. I helped myself and found a spot at one of the two long tables in the dining pavilion where we all ate.

The table was already occupied by Quentin Tupper and Wyatt Jayne. Neither of them were Snowden Family Clambake employees, though they both had business on the island. Quentin was our investor, the silent partner who'd rescued the clambake from certain bankruptcy the year before. He was a burly man, dressed as he was every day in the summer, in a blue cotton dress shirt, khaki shorts and boat shoes.

Wyatt was the architect he'd recommended to oversee the renovation of Windsholme. She looked pretty and professional in a colorful summer shift, every long, shiny brunette hair in place, despite having arrived on the island in Quentin's sailboat. By coincidence, she and I had gone to prep school together fifteen years earlier. That hadn't gotten us off to a good start. Our history had been rocky, but we were past that now. Wyatt was on the island to work on the plans for the renovation. Quentin was along to "help out."

Mom sat next to me and dug into her meal. She closed her eyes and sighed. "So good." She was blonde and petite. People said I looked like her.

"The best, Mrs. S," Mary Carey said. "Livvie sure can cook." Mary taught third grade at Busman's Harbor Elementary, and had supplemented her income by waitressing at the clambake every summer for years.

Mom smiled. "I'm lucky that way."

"How was Mrs. H's memorial? I wanted to go but—" Mary had come to work instead.

"She was the loveliest person," Leila Caspari said. She sat to the right of her best friend Mary, like always.

"Such a character," Livvie said. "The wigs! A different crazy style and color for every day of the week." As she'd entered her nineties, Heloise had dealt with her thinning hair by adopting the wildest set of wigs any of us had ever seen.

All other conversation ceased. Everyone at the long table was listening.

"You know, she went to Kim's Beauty Salon every week for years," someone said. "When she went to the wigs, she didn't want Kim to lose out on the income, so she sent a wig over to her once a week to be styled. She told Kim to be as creative as she wanted."

"And Kim was." Mom smiled, remembering.

"Those wigs came from a really expensive store in Boston," Leila told us. "When I had my cancer,

Lou sent me there. She called ahead and told them to give me whichever one I wanted and she'd pay for it."

Everyone was quiet. We all remembered Leila's cancer.

"She didn't even know me," Leila continued. "My uncle used to plow her driveway. He was so worried she'd fall, he'd shovel her steps and her walk right down to the concrete. She'd come out to chat while he worked, all bundled up. One time she asked him why he looked so worried and he told her I was sick. That was all it took."

"She was like that," Mary agreed.

"Yes, always," Mom said.

There was another moment of silence as people thought about all Heloise Herrickson had done. She'd given generously to the institutions summer people supported—the Botanical Garden, the Historical Society, and her special passion, the Art League. But there'd also been many small acts of personal charity, like Leila's wig. More than any of us knew.

"And the memorial?" Mary asked.

"It was lovely, absolutely lovely," Mom said. "Exactly as she would have wanted." I noticed Mom didn't mention that Bartholomew Frick, the only relative and heir, had been late, and rude, and hadn't spoken about his great aunt. Or talked to anyone for that matter.

But that didn't mean he wasn't the immediate focus of the conversation. "I wonder if he'll keep that old mansion?" Mary said.

"And will he keep Mrs. Fischer?" Leila asked. Ida

Fischer had been Lou Herrickson's housekeeper
forever. I'd noticed that she and Bartholomew Frick
hadn't greeted each other or spoken while on the
boat. Ida had huddled with her good friends, our
neighbors, the Snugg sisters, and Frick had kept to
himself.

"What mansion?" Wyatt asked, eyes bright.

"Herrickson House," my mother answered. "It's
a huge old thing overlooking Sea Glass Beach.
Quentin can sail you by it. It's always reminded me
a little of Windsholme. Same era, I think and I've
heard maybe even the same architect. It's been in
Francis Herrickson's family for generations. No
one thought Lou would like it there. She's from
Philadelphia originally and met Frank when she
lived in Palm Beach. But she adopted the house
and the town as if they were her own. She loved
that old place."

"The grandnephew will probably sell it to a developer who'll tear it down and build ten houses
for summer people," my brother-in-law Sonny
said. "Lotta land there. All with sea views. Has to
be worth a fortune."

"Maybe the land's protected because of Herrickson Point Light?" Leila suggested. "I think it
has some kind of historical designation."

"Frank Herrickson's great-grandfather was the
lighthouse keeper," Mom told Wyatt. "That's why
they bought the land. And then, when the U.S.
government declared the lighthouse excess, they
bought it, too."

"We can hope Frick keeps it as it is," Mary responded.

"If it was really designed by Henry Gilbert, we have to get inside," Wyatt said.

"We can ask Mr. Frick when he's a little more settled," Mom assured her.

Based on what I'd seen that morning, I was skeptical Bartholomew Frick would be open to the idea of strangers tramping through his house inspecting the moldings.

Sonny and his crew bused their dishes and headed back to the clambake fire. I stood as well. "Back to work," I announced. "There's another group due here in forty-five minutes."

One by one we went off to ready our stations and do it all again.

CHAPTER 2

I was in the Snowden Family Clambake office on the second floor of my mother's house bright and early the next morning. Mom had been in the kitchen when I came through her always-unlocked back door. She pointed toward the half-full coffee pot on the counter while barely looking up from the *Busman's Harbor Gazette*. I poured a cup and went up the back stairs.

I loved my mornings in the office, a pause to get the day organized before the craziness began. The office had been my father's before it was mine and still held his big mahogany desk, metal filing cabinets, and prints of ships on the high seas on the walls. I'd thought about changing the decor, making it more my own, but I wasn't ready to let go of Dad, even though he'd been dead for six years. As long as his things were in that room, he was there, too, guiding me through the day-to-day decisions that meant success or failure, good or bad experiences for our guests, and a livelihood for our employees and my family.

I drifted to the three big front windows in the office and looked out, down over Main Street, past the Snuggles Inn across the street and onto the pier where our ticket kiosk was already open for the day. The sun was out, bathing the town in the bright, flat light that had led so many artists to Maine. The sea was calm. It was a perfect day for a clambake. The tide was coming in, as I'd suspected. When you live near the water and make your living on it, the tides become as internalized as the time.

The tide meant I could call the clammers who sold us our steamers, the soft-shell clams that were an integral part of the clambake meal. Those clammers who didn't double as lobstermen would be at home, not out on the beaches at work. We bought the lobsters for the bake from the co-op. I could have bought our clams the same way, but I spread our business around to several local clammers, cutting out the middleman to put a little more money in their pockets and a tiny bit of savings in ours. I dialed Will Orsolini first.

"Will here."

It was a routine call. Will had delivered three fifty-pound bushels of clams to us every day since we'd opened in June without a hitch. But I'd been taught to check and double-check by my father. "Never assume," he'd said, "because when you assume, you make . . ." etc., etc.

"Hi Will. Julia Snowden. I'm calling to check on

deliveries for today. We've got a full house once again. It's been a good season."

"Julia, I was just about to call you. I got nothing for you today."

"What? Is everything okay? Are you hurt?" Raking steamers was backbreaking work and it wasn't unusual for clammers to be injured. But normally Will would have called to give a heads up if he wasn't going out.

"No. Nothing—when—Herrickson Point—morning—chain link gate—end of the access road—not letting anybody on the beach."

"What? I can't hear you. There's a lot of noise in the background. Who's not letting anybody on the beach?"

"Is that better?" He'd obviously moved the phone closer to his mouth. He didn't wait for my response before he continued. "Frickin' Frick, that's who. I'm still at the Point. There's a bunch of people here trying to get on the beach. Not just clammers. It's getting kind of ugly." He was quiet for a moment and I could hear angry shouts in the background. "Call some of the guys who clam over on Keyport Beach. They should be able to cover you. Sorry to let you down."

"It's not your fault," I said. "Take care of yourself. It sounds like it could get nasty out there."

"Already has," he answered. "Already has."

Will was right. A few of the clammers who worked Keyport Beach were able to fill my order and were happy to help. All of them had heard about the fuss at Herrickson Point and a couple said they were headed over there to see what was going on.

A quick glance at my phone told me I had time to check it out before I had to be on the boat to the clambake. I was curious, and concerned about my clam supply. I pulled my ancient maroon Chevy Caprice out of Mom's garage where I kept it. The car had been meant as a winter beater, a vehicle to brave the ice and snow and salt on Maine roads, so cheap it would be abandoned as soon as it needed a major repair, or even a minor one. But the car had failed to die with the season, and I was bent on running it into the ground.

The ride took me out of town, over the bridge onto Thistle Island and out to the farthest point of land on its opposite side. Herrickson Point was hard to miss. There were twenty or so cars and pickups parked along Rosehill Road, which dead-ended just past the turnoff to the beach. A large knot of people milled around the entrance to the turnoff. I pulled the Caprice behind the last truck and hurried over to the beach access road.

Or more correctly, the beach "no access" road. A shiny, new, ten-foot chain link gate blocked the road. High on it was a sign in large black letters that said KEEP OUT—PRIVATE PROPERTY.

The crowd was revved up. "Let us through. It's our right!" a man yelled.

"This is an outrage," an older woman carrying a beach chair shouted. When I got closer I realized she was the deeply tanned woman who'd been at Lou's memorial.

The crowd began to chant, "Let us in! Let us in! Let us in!" More than a dozen people held clam rakes aloft, moving them up and down in time to the words. The rakes had short wooden handles with curved tines and wire baskets at the end. The crowd looked like an angry mob carrying pitch-forks. Will Orsolini was at the front near the fence.

I worked my way to him. "What's going on?"

Will squinted into the sun behind me, his dark eyebrows drawn over his bright blue eyes. "Put this up overnight. I was here practically until sunset yesterday."

Obviously then, it had been planned well in advance, even though there had been no notice. "Can he do that?" I asked.

"He thinks he can."

I peered through the fence. The beach access road and parking lot ran from where I stood about two hundred yards to the end of the point where the buildings that made up Herrickson Point Light stood on the rocks. There was the light itself, tall and white-washed, a two-story keeper's house, and an outbuilding where the light's fuel had been stored back in the days when it had been lit by oil. To the left of the parking lot was a crescent of sandy beach. Sea Glass Beach wasn't wide, and it wasn't entirely sand. Boulders were strewn about both on the beach and in the water, but it was a long stretch for this part of Maine. Well back from the parking lot, up on a bluff, was Herrickson House, a shingled mansion loaded with turrets, balconies, and porches.

"This isn't what Lou would have wanted," I said to Will.

"No. She was a nice lady. I'm sorry we weren't at the memorial yesterday. I had to work and so did Nikki."

"I'm sure Lou would have understood," I assured him.

"You're right. I used to take her clams from time to time as a way to say thank you for letting us use the beach. Just enough for her and the house-keeper. Lou was always grateful and said so. She wasn't stuck up in the least."

A *woop-woop* sounded behind us as a police car made its way through the crowd. It stopped in the middle of the road and my childhood friend Jamie Dawes got out. He stood for a moment, assessing, and then made his way toward Will and me.

"I'd ask, 'what seems to be the problem,' but I think I can guess." He smiled while his eyes traveled up the fence.

"He can't keep us out, can he?" a clammer asked.

"I don't know," Jamie answered. "Why don't you folks take off and I'll go up to the house to see what he has to say?"

"We'll wait," Will responded for everyone.

Jamie shrugged. "Suit yourselves. But don't make any trouble, and absolutely no destruction of property." He looked meaningfully at the gate. Then he scaled the boulder next to the fence pole, as sure-footed as a mountain goat. He ducked around the pole, jumped off the rock, and trudged toward Herrickson House. The crowd, so raucous only moments before, watched in silence as the door opened and Jamie disappeared inside.

I checked my phone. I had to leave in ten minutes if I wanted to make it to the boat in time. The Caprice was still the last in the line of parked cars, well clear of Jamie's cruiser in the middle of the road. I should have gone while the getting was good, but I wanted to know the end of the story.

At that moment, the biggest RV I'd ever seen in motion rumbled down the road and stopped behind the police car. The door opened and a man got out. He was short, with a fringe of white hair around his bald head. When his feet hit the ground after leaving the RV's lower step, he looked at the crowd, hiking up his madras slacks. He walked purposefully toward Will and me. "You in charge here?" he asked.

I could see why he assumed it. We were standing at the front of the crowd, and Jamie, the obvious authority figure, was inside the mansion.

"Not us." Will gestured with his arm, sweeping it across the entire group of angry, chattering people. "We're trying to figure out what's going on like everybody else."

"Have you figured any of it?" The man smiled when he said it, but there was tension in his voice.

"Nope. I clam here low tide near every day, usually twice a day," Will answered. "Got here this morning and found this gate and sign." He jerked his thumb toward the gate.

"The owner of the land died recently," I added.

"She always welcomed access to the beach and the lighthouse, but it appears maybe her heir isn't so accommodating."

"Oh, we know about the death of Mrs. Herrickson." The man stuck his hand out. "Glen Barnard," he said.

Will shook first. "Willis Orsolini."

I gave him a quizzical look. I'd always assumed his full name was William. "Julia Snowden." I took the man's outstretched hand and shook.

The man turned toward the RV, cupped his hands around his mouth and yelled. "Anne, we have a situation."

A trim, white-haired woman opened the door to the RV and stood on the top step. "A what?" It wasn't until I saw her that I realized they were the couple in the lighthouse sweatshirts at Lou's memorial service the day before.

The man waved her over. There was no use shouting above the restless crowd. She worked her way toward us. "The access road and parking lot have been blocked," he said when she reached us. He explained what we'd told him.

"But we have a reservation. We paid a deposit," she said.

Lou rented the keeper's cottage to a few lucky folks every summer. The reservations were coveted and hard to get. Lighthouse lovers, and just plain lovers, from all over North America and sometimes even farther away, entered a lottery in March and ten lucky winners got a week each over the summer. The cost was nominal. Lou told people around town she did it to have a reason to keep the cottage comfortably furnished and in good repair.

"I imagine you'll have to speak to Mrs. Herrickson's grandnephew about honoring your reservation," I told them.

"What's his deal?" the man asked.

"His name is Bartholomew Frick. I don't really know him. He was at the memorial service."

"The je—guy with the Porsche?" I could tell Glen had almost said, "jerk." I didn't disagree.

Jamie emerged from the house and made the long walk down the drive. He climbed up onto the boulder he'd scaled to get in. "Listen up," he said. He stayed up the rock, speaking from above our heads. Jamie and I are the same age, thirty-one, and he was the newest member of the Busman's Harbor PD, but his height and his deep, resonant voice conveyed a sense of authority that extended beyond his uniform. The crowd quieted.

"I spoke to Mr. Frick. He has a number of documents up there and claims to have the legal right to block access to the beach. I'm not a lawyer. Someone smarter than me is going to have to sort this out." He shifted his weight to steady himself on the rock. "You should all go home, or back to your hotels, or wherever you came from. There will be no using the beach today."

There was grumbling. Some of the people at the back turned away, but the little knot of people around me didn't move.

"Tide's too high anyway," Will said. "Today is lost."

I looked at my phone. I had to get going. "That's Officer Dawes," I said to the couple from the RV. "Speak to him about your reservation. He may be willing to go back and ask Mr. Frick about it."

"Thank you," the man said, clasping my arm. "I can't tell you how much this means to us."

"Bye. Good luck." I ran for my car.

CHAPTER 3

At ten o'clock that night, after I'd returned to the harbor on the *Jacquie II* along with our dinner guests, I sat on the broken-down couch in my apartment over Gus's restaurant and opened my laptop. Chris was still at his job as a bouncer at Crowley's, Busman's Harbor's most raucous, touristy bar. After the lights in the bar came up at 1:00 AM, he'd ferry drunks back to their hotels and rental houses in the taxi he owned. In a bigger town, people might wonder if there was a conflict of interest when the bouncer who'd taken their car keys showed up later that night in the cab he owned, ready to drive them home. But in a seasonal resort, everyone worked three jobs when they could in order to get through the long winters. Most people understood and were grateful for the ride. Chris's primary business was landscaping, caring for summer people's homes. During the season all three jobs kept him hopping.

I should have gone to bed. I had work in the

morning, as I did seven days a week during tourist season. With Sea Glass Beach closed, I had to get in to the office early to ensure I had enough steamers for our two fully booked clambake meals that day. Every restaurant in town would be competing for a diminished supply.

But I was determined to stay up until Chris got home. That afternoon, for the first time ever, he'd gone to visit his older brother, Terry, who was incarcerated in the Maine State Prison in Warren, and had been for close to ten years. When the *Jacquie II* had sailed past Dinkum's Light, my phone had downloaded the texts and e-mails that had been waiting for me all day. There was a text from Chris saying he was back in Busman's Harbor and had returned to work, but other than that I hadn't heard anything.

My fingers lingered over the keyboard of my laptop. Could Bartholomew Frick really keep everyone off the beach at Herrickson Point? I'd been puzzling about it all day. It was private property, but Mrs. Herrickson had allowed access to Sea Glass Beach and the lighthouse all my life, maybe longer. I tapped a few words into a search engine.

What I discovered was eye-opening.

Unlike most other ocean-bordering states, Maine property owners did not own to the high watermark. Instead, benefiting from a Colonial Ordinance issued in the 1640s to the Massachusetts Bay Colony, of which Maine was then a part, Maine property extended to the mean low tide mark. The Ordinance was intended to encourage the colonists to build wharves. I didn't know if it had worked back then, but centuries of lawsuits and confusing court decisions had followed.

There was an exception in the ordinance: the land between the tides could be freely used for fishing, fowling, and navigation. In court decisions, fishing had been interpreted broadly to include clamming, and other kinds of foraging that resulted in edible seafood. Fowling, on the other hand, had been interpreted narrowly, to mean only bird hunting, not bird watching. Navigation definitely didn't mean you could pull up in a boat and picnic on someone's beach.

So there was, perhaps, hope for Will, though according to what I read, he couldn't cross the Herrickson's upland holdings to get to the tidal zone, and their upland holdings included the parking lot and access road. Will would have to load his clam rake, shovel, buckets, and such into a boat at a public ramp and then motor it around to Herrickson's Point to do his clamming. Did he have a boat? Most, but not all, clammers did.

That the Herricksons had allowed people to park in the lot and use the beach for decades didn't seem to make a difference. I wondered if there'd been any type of easement or other requirement for access when the Herricksons bought the lighthouse from the government, but my search engine didn't find me the answer.

My head hurt and my eyes kept closing. It was one thirty, and I couldn't wait for Chris any longer. As I powered off the laptop, I heard the outside back door to Gus's restaurant open, followed by Chris's familiar tread on the stairs to the apartment.

"Hey," I called.

"You're still up."

"I thought you might need to talk. How did today go?" My heart felt a pinch of pain when I saw the slump in his shoulders and the puffiness under his deep-set green eyes.

He let out a long sigh and crossed the studio to the alcove where our clothes were stored. He put his wallet and keys on top of the bureau, as he did every night, the precise habits of a man who had spent his previous summers living on a sailboat where everything had its place. "Okay, I guess," he answered, not looking at me.

"How did your brother seem?" It was the most neutral question I could think of in a topic that was a psychological minefield for him, and terra incognito for me.

Chris sat next to me on the couch and pulled me to him. The way he held me, resting on his side, was intimate, but it also kept me facing out, away from him, away from looking into his eyes. "He seemed the same. Which was weird, considering I haven't seen him for almost ten years. And he's in prison."

"Was he surprised to see you?"

"No, they'd told him I was coming. He didn't say it, but I think he was glad."

"And were you able to get past—"

Chris cut me off. "We didn't talk about the past." Evidently, Chris and I weren't going to, either.

"Did you ask him about Emmy?" I wasn't going to let him shut me out entirely.

Emmy Bailey was the mother of Vanessa, my ten-year-old niece Page's best friend. Vanessa had the most amazing green eyes, exactly the same as Chris's. He didn't see himself in her, but swore she was the image of his mother. Emmy, who worked at the clambake, was vague about Vanessa's origins. Her baby Luther was her son with her ex-husband Art, but Vanessa had come long before they married. The product of a one-night stand was all Emmy would say. Chris was convinced his brother was Vanessa's father. He was so convinced, he'd gone to Warren to visit his brother in the Maine State Penitentiary, even though they hadn't spoken in years.

"He said he could've known Emmy. Could've slept with her. She was in the right place at the right time, a time when he wasn't with anybody specific. But he didn't remember her. Her name didn't ring a bell and he didn't recall her when I described her."

"So we're—"

"Exactly where we were before." He paused. "I'm going to ask Terry to take a DNA test." I shifted around to face him. When I was silent he said, "You don't think I should."

"You'd have to get Emmy to allow Vanessa to take one, too. Emmy has never shown the slightest interest."

Chris paused, acknowledging the challenge. "I can convince her."

We were quiet again. I'd never understood why Vanessa's paternity was so important to Chris—why it had compelled him to heal the breach with his brother, take a day off during the season to travel to the prison, or why he was considering trying to convince a woman to help prove a paternity she didn't seem to care about. When I'd asked him in the past, he'd said, "Because it's the right thing."

I supposed it was the right thing. Vanessa had a right to know. She would certainly ask at some point. Maybe Terry had a right to know, too. His sentence was ending soon. But there had to be more to it for Chris to be so invested in a matter didn't directly involve him.

I'd learned to tread lightly. It wasn't that Chris didn't want to tell me. I was convinced he could only handle the subject so much at a time himself. Today, he'd handled a lot. We were both tired. It was way past time for bed.

CHAPTER 4

I called Will as soon as I got into my office the next morning. He reported the chain link gate was still blocking the road at Herrickson Point and he had nothing for me. I asked him to call if anything changed.

I worried about the clam supply. Steamers were an important part of the clambake meal. Some people loved them more than the lobsters. Every restaurant in town would be scrambling to make sure they had enough.

Luckily, the clambake's resources were deep and I was able to line up the clams we needed. I made the rest of my calls and checked on the state of our reservations. They were still going strong. We had two tour bus groups for lunch today in addition to our other customers. My phone told me it was nine thirty. Still plenty of time until the boat. I took off for the police station.

There I got lucky. Jamie was plucking at the computer at one of the two desks Busman's Harbor's seven sworn officers shared. "Here comes Trouble," he said when he saw me. But he smiled when he said it.

"I just spoke to Will Orsolini," I said after I greeted him. "He told me the beach road at Herrickson Point is still fenced off."

"Yup. The town has filed an injunction, so that may change in the next few days, but that's the way it's going to be for now."

"We have a short summer season," I pointed out. "Not many days to go to the beach." He nodded. Of course he understood. Except for college, he'd been in Busman's Harbor all his life.

"I hear you, but it's a complex situation."

"How does Frick even have the right to do this, so soon after Lou's death? Her estate can't have gone through probate yet."

"Apparently, Frick is both the 'Responsible Person,' as we call executors in Maine, as well as the heir. He's claiming that he's protecting the property as the executor."

"At least the clammers should be able to access the beach. They have the right for fishing, fowling, and navigation," I pointed out.

"I see you've read up on the Ordinance of 1640, too. The clammers may have that right, but they have no right to cross the road or parking lot, which are clearly on the Herrickson property. Let the court do its work, Julia. If they decide for the town, we'll enforce the law, believe me."

I got up to leave. "Were you able to help those people out, the ones who paid to stay in the keeper's cottage at Herrickson Point Light?"

"Not yet. Nice couple. I sent them over to
Glooscap. They had one space left."

Camp Glooscap was a local RV park. Its new
owners were doing well with it.

"Okay, thanks," I said, but I didn't leave.

Jamie looked up from his computer. "Julia, what
are you thinking? This isn't your problem to solve.
You understand that, right?"

"It's my problem if I don't have clams at the
height of the season," I reminded him.

"Julia—"

His voice held a warning, but I was out the door.

What I was thinking was the legal process would
grind slowly. Meanwhile, Will's family would suffer,
and so would the families of many other clammers.

Jamie's talk with Frick the day before must have
been hurried, the tone influenced by the chanting
crowd at the gate. Maybe no one had taken the
time to tell Bartholomew Frick about the impor-
tance of the beach to the town. Perhaps a calm,
reasoned discussion could accomplish what in-
junctions and angry mobs could not.

I parked the Caprice on Rosehill Road across
from the upper gates to Herrickson House. The
long driveway that wound from the beach parking
lot to the mansion was not how the residents of the
house came and went. Instead, they used the two
side entrances, where I was parked now, farther up
Rosehill Road and closer to the house. A long,

electronically operated gate guarded the drive that led to the two-story garage behind the house. Next to it, a pedestrian gate led to a path that ran parallel to the drive until it veered off to the house. A tall, neatly trimmed boxwood hedge stood along Rosehill Road, blocking access along the rest of the property line.

The big car gate had a keypad, but no sign of a doorbell or speaker system. I pushed it, but it didn't budge.

I had higher hopes for the pedestrian gate. It was waist-high, painted a soft blue. A trellis arched over it, training the rosebushes for which the road was named.

I pushed. Nothing. I reached over the gate to feel for a latch but felt only a lock with a place for a key, identical to the side I was on. I pulled. Nothing.

If I wanted to reach Herrickson House, I was going to have to go in the way Jamie had. I left the Caprice parked on the road and walked toward the beach.

As Will had told me, the chain link gate still barred the way. All was quiet for now. No crowd was gathered. I stood on the road and studied the sign—KEEP OUT. I'm a rule-follower by nature, but I put on hand on the boulder beside the gate post, hoisting myself up and over, the same way Jamie had gone the day before. He's a foot taller than me and I had to scramble, but I made it.

From the top of the rock I climbed down the other side, which put me in the beach parking lot.

I followed it until I came to the long driveway lined with finely broken seashells that led up the hill to Herrickson House.

Mom had said Herrickson House and the mansion on our island, Windsholme, were of the same era, perhaps even the same architect. Both had stone foundations, shingle sides, and towering chimneys. But while Windsholme stood strong and straight against the Atlantic, a miracle of balance and proportion, Herrickson House was all balconies and turrets, nooks and crannies. Both houses were impressive, but while Windsholme was a stately grand dame, Herrickson House was a debutante in a frilly party dress.

I squared my shoulders. I'd never felt intimidated by the outside of the house when Lou lived there, but she didn't anymore. Despite the bright sun, or maybe because of the shadows it cast on the deep, irregular crevices, the house radiated a menacing darkness.

I put one foot in front of the other and marched up the driveway, holding my head high and trying to project the attitude I had every right to be there. As I climbed onto the porch, my chest tightened. But really what was the worst Frick could do, yell at me? I'd been yelled at by better people.

I'd taken two steps across the porch when the front door banged open. Ida Fischer, Lou's longtime housekeeper, stomped onto the porch, carrying a giant handbag. She looked me up and down. "He's in the study. I'd announce you, but I've quit."

My mouth dropped open. I tried to shut it to say some words, but couldn't manage it.

"Good luck with whatever it is you've come to talk to him about. He is the most odious person I have ever had the displeasure of meeting. I've left a note, but if he wonders where I am, feel free to tell him I'm no longer in his employ. If anyone's looking to reach me, I'll be at my sister's."

"Are you sure?" I stammered.

"I am. That awful man shouldn't be allowed to live in this magnificent house."

Her voice caught on the final words, and I realized how hard it must be for her losing Lou. They'd been together, the two of them, day in and day out for decades. I put a hand out to pat her upper arm. When I did, she put her hand over mine, and said, "Thank you." She gave her head a small shake, and then climbed down the steps.

I watched her as she marched down the path that led to the pedestrian gate, her enormous handbag swinging from her crooked elbow. When she reached the gate, she jerked it toward her. Evidently a key wasn't needed to open it from the inside. In a flash, she was out on Rosehill Road, climbing into an old brown Toyota I hadn't seen arrive. The car took off and she was gone.

CHAPTER 5

The front door was still wide open as Ida Fischer had left it. I stuck my head into the front reception room and called, "Mr. Frick? Bartholomew?"

The sound of my voice echoed through the big house, but no one responded. I took a cautious step inside. I'd never been inside Herrickson House before.

The first reception room was large and light-filled, with a grand staircase coming down the far wall, just like Windsholme, but here the room was oval-shaped, with smooth walls in a fine-grained, light wood and an inglenook under the center of the stairs. On the floor, an oval Oriental rug fit perfectly, leaving a couple of feet of polished wood flooring around its edge. In the center of the room was an oval table, and on it a large, oval glass bowl. The bowl was empty, but I imagined it had held flowers when Lou reigned.

There was a piece of white stationery on the

table. I didn't even have to get close to it to snoop. I QUIT, it said in big block letters. WILL COME BACK FOR MY THINGS. IDA FISCHER.

"Mr. Frick! Bartholomew Frick!" I shouted louder, trying to make sure he knew I was there. Given how he felt about having people on his property, I was sure he wouldn't be a fan of me wandering in his house.

I took another few steps. To my left, an archway opened into an enormous living room. I walked through the opening and stopped. The room was amazing, and pure Lou. There was art from every era of human history on the walls, huge abstracts in dazzling colors, medium-sized landscapes with milkmaids and shepherds, large photographs, painted miniatures, and tiny cut silhouettes. It was crazy and should have looked awful, but somehow it was wonderful, and so much like Lou, who had loved the visual arts above all things and who had been an artist herself.

I walked fully into the room, was pulled into it really, by its dazzling display. The furniture was mid-century modern, including the long leather sofa, but didn't look out of place in the Victorian era house. The built-in bookshelves and occasional tables were crowded with framed photographs, from old black and white ones, right up through Lou's hundredth birthday party the previous year. On the other side of the room were two doorways, one on either side of the fireplace. I kept going. "Mr. Frick! Bartholomew!"

I chose the doorway to the left of the hearth, though it turned out it didn't matter, both doors led to a long room with three walls of windows. The room was dominated by a tall desk full of pigeon-holes and drawers. Bartholomew Frick stood in front of it, squinting in concentration at a yellowed piece of paper covered in brown script.

I cleared my throat. "Mr. Frick."

"Yikes!" He straightened up so quickly he almost jumped. "Do you always sneak up on people? Why didn't that woman announce you?"

"I'm sorry, I didn't mean to startle you. Mrs. Fischer isn't here." It was a deliberately ambiguous answer. Let him find the note. I wasn't going to be the one to break it to him. "I'm Julia Snowden. We met yesterday on my tour boat."

He ignored my outstretched hand, folded the paper he'd been reading, put it in a yellowed envelope, and dropped it on a pile of similar envelopes on the desk. It only took him a few seconds, but I felt like a fool with my hand out.

He rolled down the top of the desk, finally reaching for my hand. "Bartholomew Frick," he said. "Call me Bart. What brings you here?"

"This place is amazing," I said.

"You've never been here?" he asked.

"Never inside."

"Come. Let's walk. As long as you're here, you may as well see it."

I was surprised by the invitation. He didn't seem like the awful man Ida had described, the man who'd put up the fence.

He started toward the archway to the living room, leading me through it, back to the entry hall. If he saw Ida Fischer's note on the table, he ignored it, moving me toward the dining room, which showed the same exuberant mix of decoration as the living room. A modern glass dining table surrounded by mismatched chairs from the last three centuries stood at the room's center. Beneath the table was an orange shag carpet, which somehow worked in the room. As in the other spaces, the walls were crowded with art, from African masks to American folk art to antique maps. It was like a museum. Not an antiseptic museum with lots of white walls and fancy lighting, but a Victorian's idea of a museum, like the Isabella Stewart Gardner Museum in Boston.

"The art is amazing," I said.

He grunted in response and kept walking.

"My family has a home from the same era," I said, trying to find a neutral topic. "My mom believes they were designed by the same architect, Henry Gilbert." I hadn't been able to see a resemblance from the outside, but inside, Herrickson House felt strangely familiar.

"Umph." He looked me over again. He hadn't considered I might own a mansion. Of course, I didn't. My mother did, and it was abandoned and partially destroyed, but I wasn't going to tell him that.

"My family is having our home restored. Our architect said she'd love to come over to check Herrickson House out."

He grunted something noncommittal that sounded like, "We'll see."

We kept walking through rooms full of Greek and Roman sculpture, antiques, and collections in

glass cases—butterflies, coins, and stamps. The
size and breadth of it was astonishing. The stuff
had to be worth millions. I knew Lou was rich, of
course, but I hadn't realized she was rich-rich.

As we entered the next room, a breakfast room
with breathtaking views of the Atlantic, an oil
painting dancing with bright colors caught my eye.
"Is that one of your aunt's?" I pointed.

"One of 'em. There are, like, fifty in her studio.
I'm not sure what I'll do with 'em. Probably have
to burn them."

My heart sank. "Lou was quite well known around
here. Her paintings are in a lot of homes. I'm sure
you could sell them. Or donate them to a charity
that would auction them."

He stopped abruptly. It was the first time during
the visit I'd disagreed with him, and like back on
the pier when I told him he'd have to move his
Porsche, he didn't take it well. "Why did you say
you were here?"

It was do or die time. "I didn't. I came today because I want to talk to you about the beach and the
access road."

I had his attention, but not in a good way. "That
subject is closed."

"Is it? Because as I'm sure you know the town
has filed for an injunction. If you understood how
important the beach is to the clammers, the
tourists, and the locals, who like to swim and sun at
the end of a long day, too."

He pushed a hand through his abundant brown
hair. "I have no objection to them doing any of
those things. Just not on my property."

"But your aunt always—"

"Great-aunt-in-law," he corrected. "Lou was my grandmother's brother's wife, whom he married late in life. They had no children. Herrickson House belongs to the Herricksons, of which my grandmother was one. They'll be no more tromping around on the property by strangers."

"We weren't strangers to your aunt."

"You're strangers to me, and based on this encounter and others of its ilk, my intention is to keep it that way. I may have to live here, but I don't have to mix."

I'd been trying to help and I'd made things worse. Ida Fischer was right. He was odious. "What about those poor people who paid to spend the night in the keeper's cottage at Herrickson Point Light?" I said. "They gave your aunt a deposit. They have a right to be here."

"I offered to refund their money, in cash. That they refused is no concern of mine. I trust you can see yourself out."

Out on the front porch, I checked my phone. Five minutes after eleven. I'd have to hustle to drive back to town and make it to the *Jacquie II*. I followed the path Ida Fischer had taken to the upper gate. It clicked open and I stepped through it onto the grassy strip that ran along Rosehill Road.

"Can you leave that open?"

The voice, a husky smoker's rasp, came from across the lane. The deeply tanned woman I'd seen at Lou's memorial and again in the crowd at the blocked parking lot came out through a gate on the other side of the road.

I hesitated, my hand on the Herricksons' gate. Should I let her in? While I dithered, she hurried across the lane and took the gate from me, rendering the decision unnecessary on my part.

"Do you want to speak to Mr. Frick?" I asked.

"Is he there?"

"Yes. But he's not open to discussing beach access if that's what you're hoping." She looked crestfallen. "The town is bringing an injunction to force him to take the gate down," I told her.

Up close, she showed every bit of her age, which I guessed to be around seventy. The sun had made her skin leathery, a look you saw in Maine mostly on fishermen and farmers. Her hair was long and white with a streak of blonde in it, tied in a ponytail she'd looped through the back of a pink baseball hat. She wore an open lace cover-up over a relatively small bathing suit, given her age. Her skin glowed bright white at the suit's edges.

"I'd hoped he was making a point, asserting his right, for legal reasons or whatever, and would open it back up after twenty-four hours," she said.

"No such luck. I'm Julia Snowden, by the way."

"I remember you from the boat. Vera French."

"Were you close to Lou?"

She hesitated. "No." She drew the word out, as if she was making up her mind how to characterize their relationship. "I've been her neighbor for more than twenty years. I thought it was the right thing to go to her memorial."

Rosehill Road was lined on the other side with the same type of high boxwood hedge that bordered the Herrickson estate. Peeking above the hedge was a gray-shingled dormer and the worn roof of a cottage smaller than Herrickson House, but of the same era. Modest as the cottage appeared to be, its property ran all the way down to the ocean. It would have its own magnificent views.

In the tall hedge was a wooden pedestrian gate not unlike the Herricksons', though Vera's was painted bright green. It had rosebushes trained over its trellis, too, and a distinctive crescent shape cut into the top of its door.

"I'm sure it was the right thing," I assured her. "It was nice to meet you."

"Nice to meet you, too." Vera stepped onto the Herrickson property. "Even if he won't be reasonable about the beach, I'd still like to meet Bartholomew Frick. And I've never been inside the house." She waved, then bent to the ground and picked up a good-sized gray rock, positioning it to prop the gate open. "In case I need to escape in a hurry." Her deep voice made her laugh sound like a seal's bark. She waved good-bye and disappeared down the path.

I started toward the Caprice. If I didn't get a move on, I was going to miss my boat. As I did, I glanced to where Rosehill Road dead-ended a few yards beyond the turnoff to the beach access road. A dark red pickup was parked at the farthest point, practically on the rocks. Behind it was an empty boat trailer with a Maine plate.

Had it been there before? I was positive it hadn't. Despite the time, I walked down to check it out.

When I got closer I could see that as I'd suspected, it was Will Orsolini's truck. So he did have a boat. Maybe he was taking it over to the beach to clam, which would be legal if I understood the 1640 Ordinance. I went back to the chain link gate and looked for him on the beach and in the water, but the cove was empty all the way to the lighthouse.

I got in my car, started her up, and pulled onto Rosehill Road. As I crested the top of the hill parallel with Herrickson House, a giant beige RV whizzed by me, headed toward the beach.

Glen and Anne Barnard, unless I missed my guess, and they sure were in a heck of hurry. If they were going to plead their case with Bart Frick to let them stay at the keeper's cottage, it was a journey that would end in disappointment.

CHAPTER 6

The afternoon flew, as it always did during our busiest times. The day was beautiful, warm with a light breeze, the sky robin's egg blue, and the Atlantic a deep navy. By the time the lunch guests, sun-drunk and full-bellied, boarded the *Jacquie II*, I was hungry. Livvie and her kitchen crew, as always anticipating our needs, put a dozen quiches out on the bar, adding an enormous green salad and slices of watermelon.

Eager to get off my feet, I sat at one of the long tables, directly across from Emmy Bailey. Before she'd come to work for us, she'd waitressed at Crowley's in town, and struggled with childcare that had overwhelmed her ancient grandmother. Working at the clambake had solved multiple problems. Emmy brought ten-year-old Vanessa and ten-month-old Luther to the island with her, which provided my niece Page, who was at the age where living on an island all summer might seem less like an adventure and more like a sentence, with a

companion. We'd hired a pair of teenaged girls to
look after them, and most especially the babies,
Luther and Jack. Both boys were getting more mo-
bile. Luther was pulling himself up and cruising
along the picnic benches, and Jack had perfected
the art of rolling over, and over, and over.

The conversation flowed around us, most of it
the usual topics, stories of family activities, com-
ments about how lucky we'd been with the weather
this season, and so on. A discussion about the gate
barring access to Sea Glass Beach was inevitable.
For a group so diverse in age, income, education,
and political convictions, our opinions were far
more unified on this, than on any other subject.
Everyone agreed that the beach should be accessible to all, and that Bart Frick was an enormous
jerk.

Slowly people cleared their plates and went off
to prepare for our dinner guests. I started to rise
off the picnic bench when Emmy said, "Julia, do
you have a minute?"

I did. More or less a minute. I sat back down.

"Do you know why Chris keeps asking me about
Vanessa's father?"

I did, sort of. He believed his brother in prison
was Vanessa's father. I wasn't sure how much to say
to Emmy. It wasn't my story to tell. And it sounded
a little crazy.

"Why does he even care?" she asked when I didn't
respond. "I know Nessie has the green eyes, like he
does, but I've told him a thousand times, it isn't
him, if that's what he's worried about. I remember
her dad. It's just that, it was a one-time thing, and I

never found him again. Not that I was eager to. I didn't think he was good dad material."

She hesitated. I still hadn't said anything, which I would have found annoying if I was on the other side of the conversation.

"Can you ask him to stop? It's not something I'm eager to talk about. I definitely don't want Vanessa hearing about it. And, it's a little creepy, to tell you the truth."

She stopped talking then, and I couldn't blame her. When you've called someone's boyfriend a creep, what more is there to say? I smiled, to let her know I wasn't mad, and then we were both rescued by the loud whistle of the *Jacquie II* as she pulled up to our dock with our dinner guests aboard.

"I'll talk to him," I said in the most neutral tone I could manage.

I don't think anyone noticed, but I was "off" for the rest of the night. I knew my boyfriend wasn't creepy. But the truth was, I knew only slightly more than Emmy did. Chris was convinced his incarcerated brother was Emmy's father. But why did he care so much about proving it? Why did he care at all?

There had to be more to it. I wasn't looking forward to the conversation we were going to have that night.

CHAPTER 7

Bthat conversation would have to wait. When
our dinner guests lumbered off the *Jacquie II*, a
state trooper stood on the pier. Waiting for me.
This can't be good.

"Ms. Snowden? Lieutenant Binder and Sergeant
Flynn would like to speak to you at the police station."

"Why? I haven't done anything, I swear. Tell
them I've been minding my own business. Seriously." I had been to see Bart Frick that morning
about opening the beach, but that was a local matter. Why would the state police care? Why would
anyone care about me visiting that awful man?

"Ms. Snowden, I'd rather not discuss this with
you here. Let's walk." The pier was crowded, with
our dinner guests and many others strolling back
from restaurants, headed to bars, out for ice cream.
People walked by, staring, stopping their conversations so they could overhear ours.

Out of the corner of my eye, I spotted Will Orsolini and his family at Small's Ice Cream Shop on the corner where the road met the pier. It was almost ten o'clock. I would have thought it was late to have their little ones out.

Will's wife Nikki had been in the same high school class as Livvie. She was tall and pleasantly round with long, dark hair that fell over her high forehead. Their children stair-stepped down in age—six, four, and the toddler in the stroller, sticky-faced with chocolate ice cream.

Will saw me and started to wave, but then spotted the state police officer beside me. Will lowered his hand, his brows creased, lips tight with concern. I gave a little wave, meant to signal, "Everything's cool," and kept walking.

I spotted a state police cruiser about thirty feet ahead, parked on the street at the top of the pier. "I'm not going in that." I pointed to it. "The police station's a five-minute walk."

"I'll let Lieutenant Binder know you're on your way."

"Thank you." I walked with him until we got to his cruiser. Then I split off and continued up Main Street, cut across the library lawn and then its parking lot, and arrived at Busman's Harbor's ugly, brick town-hall-firehouse-police-station complex.

Inside, the place buzzed with activity, so different from when I'd visited Jamie there that morning. The civilian receptionist wasn't at her desk, her shift would have ended hours earlier. Instead, the same state trooper I'd left moments before sat in her chair. "I'll tell them you're here."

I nodded.

He disappeared into the multi-purpose room the Major Crimes Unit used when they were in town. He was only gone a few seconds. "They will see you now," he said when he returned.

Lieutenant Binder rose from behind the folding table he used as a desk. "Hello, Julia."

Sergeant Flynn stood by the opposite wall in the large room. He nodded an acknowledgment. One of the last times we'd seen one another, he'd told me he was in love with my friend Genevieve and had asked her to marry him. It was an unusual confidence. He'd barely tolerated my "help" with several of their cases up to that point. In turn, I'd told him about my love for Chris, and how it was tempered by a sense there were things about him I still didn't know. Since Genevieve had declined Flynn's proposal in order to work as a private chef on a yacht, I wondered if he felt awkward after our personal disclosures in the dark of night as we'd waited for a killer.

If Lieutenant Binder knew or sensed any of this, he ignored it. He gestured for me to sit in one of the two folding chairs in front of his table, chairs I knew from experience were impossible to get comfortable in. Flynn crossed the room and sat in the other.

"Why am I here?" I asked. "I swear, I haven't done a thing."

Binder allowed his mouth to curve into a smile under his ski-slope nose. Flynn remained stone-faced as usual. Binder glanced at his computer screen.

"We understand from Ms. Ida Fischer that you visited Bartholomew Frick this morning at his residence, Herrickson House."

"I did," I admitted.

"What time was that?" Binder continued.

"I got there around ten thirty. What is this about?"

Binder leaned back in his chair, the very picture of relaxed, casual conversation. "We'll get to that. How long were you with Mr. Frick?"

"About half an hour. Seriously, you two are freaking me out. Has something happened?"

Binder leaned forward, placing both elbows and forearms on his desk. "Mr. Frick is deceased."

I'd expected it was something serious. The Major Crimes Unit didn't come to town for trivial reasons. They didn't summon you to the police station at ten o'clock at night for a friendly chat. I had even suspected what that serious thing was, especially when the Lieutenant had asked me about Frick. But Binder's statement hit me hard. I hadn't known Frick well, and what I had known, I hadn't liked. But I had been with him that morning, talking about his great-aunt's home and her artwork. He hadn't been a nice man, but he had been a living, breathing one.

"Why did you visit Mr. Frick?" Binder asked.

I cleared my throat, which was suddenly tight. "What happened to him? What time did it happen?"

There was a long silence when none of us said anything. Then Flynn surprised me by saying, "Mr. Frick's death was unexpected and certainly caused by another person. We'd rather not go into details yet, but it is entirely possible you were the last person to see him alive aside from his killer."

A shiver ran down my spine and I hugged myself tighter.

"Why did you visit Mr. Frick?" Binder asked again, more gently this time.

"If you've been in town long enough to talk to Mrs. Fischer, you know Bart Frick put a gate across the road and is denying access to the beach and lighthouse."

Binder's light brown brows rose toward his balding dome. "You went to Herrickson House to talk to Frick about the gate?"

"I did. There'd been a lot of yelling and a legal action filed. I thought maybe no one had ever explained to him in a calm, logical way how important the beach is to the town."

Binder's face crinkled into a smile. "And you thought you were the person to do this?"

"I thought maybe if no one had tried it—" It did sound kind of arrogant when I heard him say it.

"Why is this your business?" Binder pressed.

"The steamers we serve at the clambake come from the beach he blocked off. Some of them, anyway. And the beach and lighthouse are important to tourism, and tourism is important to my business."

"How did it go?" Flynn asked.

"Not so well," I admitted. "We had a nice talk about the house. He gave me a tour to look at all the artwork and collections."

Flynn's brow creased. "He invited you upstairs to the bedroom to see his etchings?"

"No, nothing like that. But it seemed we were having a nice conversation. Until I brought up the issue of the beach."

"And then?" Binder scowled.

"And then he got furious and basically threw me out."

"You parted on bad terms," Flynn clarified.

"You could say that." There was an uncomfortable silence in the room. "I didn't kill him, if that's what you're asking."

Binder laughed. "I wouldn't dream of it."

Even Flynn cracked a smile. "But tell me, who else did you see at the beach this morning?"

I moved my brain back to the morning, picturing Herrickson House, the view down to the beach, the lighthouse and the dark blue water beyond it. "Ms. Fischer," I answered. "You already know that."

"Did you actually see Ms. Fischer leave the premises?"

I pictured her stalking out the upper gate. "Yes. She was picked up by someone in a brown car."

"Were Ms. Fischer, Mr. Frick, and the person in the brown car the only people you saw?" Binder asked.

"I didn't see the person behind the wheel of the brown car," I clarified. "When I left, I ran into Vera French, the woman who lives across Rosehill Road."

"She was in her yard?"

"She asked me to hold the Herrickson gate open so she could get onto the property."

Binder put on a pair of half glasses and typed into his laptop. "The same gate Ms. Fischer exited from?"

"Yes. It locks from the outside, but not from the inside."

"Is that how you got to Mr. Frick's house in the first place?"

It was so odd to hear it called "Mr. Frick's house." He hadn't lived in it long enough to make a mark. "I climbed over the boulder down at the beach road. I saw Officer Dawes do it yesterday."

Binder nodded. "Did this Ms. French in fact enter the property?"

"She did. Last I saw her, she was headed toward the house."

"Thanks, that helps," Binder said. "We're looking for witnesses. Anyone else?"

"When I was leaving, I saw an RV speed down the road. The people in it are called Barnard, Anne and Glen. They'd made a reservation to stay at the keeper's cottage that Frick refused to honor. Officer Dawes has been involved with them. He told me they're staying at Camp Glooscap. You can probably get their contact information from him."

"Is that it?" Binder didn't seem to suspect I was holding something back. He was trying to jog my memory.

But I was holding something back. It felt like a betrayal to say it. But I did.

"I didn't see any people. But I saw Will Orsolini's truck parked at the dead end by the water.

It had a boat trailer on the back. I thought he might be clamming in the area."

Binder asked me to spell Orsolini and wanted Will's contact info. I took out my phone and read off Will's cell number.

He rose and Flynn did, too. Binder reached across the desk and shook my hand. "Thanks, Julia. We'll let you know if we need anything else. Please call if you think of anything, or discover anything you believe could be of help to us. Anything at all."

I hesitated. "I feel badly about letting that woman through the gate." Then I remembered. "She propped it open with a rock. Do you think that how the 'other person,' as you called the killer, got in?"

Binder smiled. "Julia, in a twenty-four-hour period, you and Officer Dawes entered the property in the same manner, over the rocks. The place was hardly a fortress."

I didn't move. "I could be more helpful if you told me more. How did Frick die, exactly?"

"Thanks, Julia," Binder said firmly.

The conversation was over.

CHAPTER 8

When I left the police station, the streets had quieted. Music and light still tumbled out the doors of the bars and clubs, but even at the season's peak, Busman's Harbor was a family town and most people had found their way to their hotel rooms or summer homes for the night.

I was surprised when Will and Nikki appeared on Main Street, obviously making their way home from the pier. The four-year-old was asleep in the stroller and Will held the toddler in his arms, her head against his shoulder.

Will raised the hand that wasn't holding the child as I approached. "Hi, Julia," he called softly. The words floated on the cool night air. They waited at the corner for me to reach them. "Enjoying a night out with the family." Will inclined his head toward the sleeping toddler. "I don't need to get up early. No clamming tomorrow. We're trying to work out something with the clammers at Keyport Beach, but no deal yet. What was that about on the pier?"

He was the last person I wanted to see in that moment, asking the last question I wanted to answer. Should I tell him I'd given his name to the police? Even worse that I'd placed him near the scene of a murder?

I kept my voice low, mostly for the sleeping children, but also because I didn't want my words to be overheard. "Bart Frick was killed today at Herrickson House. I was there this morning, so the detectives wanted to find out what I knew."

"Frick is dead?" Nikki's shock mirrored how I'd felt when I got the same news.

"What happened?" Will's voice was a hoarse but urgent whisper.

"I don't know. They wouldn't give me details. But for sure it wasn't natural causes."

"I'm sorry," Will said. "I'm sorry you had to go through that."

"It wasn't so bad. It's not like I was there when it happened." It was the moment of truth. Do or die time. I plunged on. "They may want to talk to you."

"Me, why?" Will's blue eyes widened. Nikki drew in a sharp breath in surprise.

"Because I told them I saw your truck at the end of the road when I left."

Will barked a laugh. "That's all? I took the boat off Herrickson Beach to get some quahogs." Quahogs were the hard-shell clams used in chowder, baked stuffed clams, and other dishes. Unlike the soft shells we served as steamers, most quahogs lived in the water, below the low tide mark, and were often, though not always, dredged by people in boats.

"I'm sorry. They asked me who I saw. I didn't see you, but I saw your truck."

"Don't worry about it. If they ask me, I'll tell 'em."

Will's reaction was a relief. We said our good-byes and they took off in the direction of home. I walked over the harbor hill to my apartment.

But once there, I couldn't settle down. Ordinarily, I would have gone to bed, but that night, I had to find a way to tell the man I loved that he was creeping out a young woman who worked for me with his, it had to be said, obsessive interest in her daughter. Knowing he suspected she was his niece, it wasn't creepy, but I could certainly appreciate how it might feel that way to Emmy.

And something else was nagging at me as well. Something at the edge of my memory. I was sure there was something about the morning and my time inside Herrickson House that I hadn't told Binder and Flynn.

The whole visit had been odd. From climbing over the boulder to walking past the deserted beach, which should have been crowded on a beautiful day. Then being the recipient of Mrs. Fischer's resignation, followed by the tour of the mad and marvelously decorated house with Bart Frick. I searched my memory. There was something else, something else.

Then I remembered. The envelopes. The stack of yellowing envelopes he'd stood next to on the roll top desk. He'd been reading one of the letters, and my sense had been he'd hastily put it back in the envelope when he'd realized I was in the room. Why? It was his house and his stuff, presumably including the letters. But I should have mentioned his behavior to Binder or Flynn, in case it was important. At a minimum, they should look at the letters.

I was still on the couch, but my eyes were almost closed when Chris came running up the stairs.

"I heard you were met on the pier by a state policeman. Are you okay?"

The concern in his eyes melted my heart. I went to him and he folded me in his strong arms. "I'm fine. Bartholomew Frick isn't. Someone killed him at Herrickson House today."

He let go and stepped back so he could look me in the face. "Frick is dead? Did you see him? Were you there when it happened?"

"No. I did see him, but he was very much alive when I left him. Binder and Flynn heard I was there today and wanted to ask a few questions. That's all."

"Okay." He hugged me again. I felt so safe in his arms. I didn't want to break the spell, but I had to. "I stayed up because we need to talk."

"Wait. There's something else? Besides a murder?"

I led him to the couch and asked him to sit. We were both exhausted, not the best time to have a serious conversation, but the alternative was not having it at all.

"Emmy Bailey spoke to me today."

"That's nice . . ." He said the words slowly, drawing them out, making it clear he knew there was more to it.

"She's concerned about your interest in Vanessa."

"What does *that* mean?" I had his full attention.

"You've asked her a lot of questions about Vanessa, especially about who her father is. You've asked more than once."

"Julia—"

"It's not a casual conversation former co-workers have." Chris and Emmy had worked together at Crowley's before she'd moved to the clambake. "It's not something people press relative strangers about. It's not something you're entitled to know about your girlfriend's niece's best friend's absent parent."

"I haven't pressured her."

"You've asked more times than she's comfortable with."

"I want Vanessa and Terry to take DNA tests."

It wasn't the response I'd expected. "Chris!" I was tired and short-tempered. "You haven't heard a word I've said!"

"I need to know," he responded, as if it was an answer. "Vanessa will want to know when she's older."

"Then leave it to them. Terry will be out of prison before the end of the year. Let them resolve this. It really is none of your business."

He sat unmoving, his work boots firmly planted on the soft pine floors of the studio, his arms crossed over his chest. The picture of someone who wasn't going to change his mind.

The silence hung between us for a long moment.

I didn't want to ask, but I had to. "Are you worried Vanessa is yours?"

"No! Absolutely not."

I waited for him to expand his answer. He didn't. It wasn't a completely ridiculous question. Emmy claimed she remembered the other party, but admitted an alcohol and drug-fueled one-night stand that had resulted in Vanessa's birth. I was sure Chris didn't remember every encounter in his twenties, either. And there were those green, green eyes.

When it was clear he wasn't going to say more, I tried again. "You can see how it's creepy, right? A thirty-six-year-old man asking a lot of questions about a ten-year-old girl."

He got it then. He swore and dropped his head into his hands. He was mad at me, but mostly he was embarrassed. He'd been a man on a mission who hadn't stopped to think how his actions looked, how his questions made Emmy feel. I moved toward him and put a hand on his shoulder. I felt the warmth, the muscled strength. "So you see you can't ask Emmy to have Vanessa take a DNA test," I said quietly.

"You're right, I can't," he agreed. "You're going to have to do it."

CHAPTER 9

Chris was gone when I woke up the next morning. We hadn't spoken much after he'd asked me to talk to Emmy. I hadn't refused. I suspected in the near future he'd realize the inappropriateness of what he'd asked and back off. In the meantime, I had no intention of attempting to persuade Emmy, or even of raising the subject, at least until Chris answered a lot more questions. But if I didn't say no directly, it would prevent Chris from asking her, at least for a while. *What a mess.*

After I got dressed, I wandered downstairs to Gus's restaurant, which was noisy and bustling on a Saturday morning. Gus served the best breakfasts in the world, which he offered up, when he got around to you, in his own good time, to a very specific crowd. Gus served only locals. It was discriminatory, not to mention illegal, but I had come to treasure finding a pocket of space where I didn't have to be "on" for anybody. Over the past year and a half, I'd grown to love running the Snowden Family Clambake, sharing our island and traditions with people from all over the world. But I spent ten hours a day with a smile plastered on my face, dealing with the needs of customers or employees, and it was so great to drop that once in a while.

I had started toward the only empty stool at the counter, when out of the corner of my eye I spotted Lieutenant Binder seated alone in a booth, eyes glued to his phone.

He looked up as I slid in across from him. "Of all the gin joints in all the world—" he said.

"I live upstairs. It's not much of a coincidence. Did you stay in town overnight?"

"Naw. I drove back to Augusta and came back early this morning."

Binder was an exception to Gus's "locals only" rule. He'd been in town enough, I guessed, and had originally come into the restaurant accompanied by local cops. Gus's rules were hard to understand anyway. How many winters did a retiree have to spend in town before he was a local? How many generations did a summer family have to live in the harbor before they were welcome? It was all pretty arbitrary. Like many other people, I suspected it depended on how much Gus liked you.

"Make yourself at home," Binder said, after I already had. He smiled when he said it. I asked about his wife and two boys. She was with the state police, too, a motorcycle cop in the summer, in a cruiser in some pretty remote areas of the state the rest of the year. The duel careers put stress on their home life, but they seemed to manage pretty well.

"How do you think Flynn is doing?" I asked after Binder filled me in on his family's activities.

"You mean after having his heart broken?" Binder shrugged. "Pretty well I think. His head's in the job. He's back at the gym."

I couldn't imagine Flynn, of the toned body, had ever skipped the gym. He must have been hurting.

Binder asked after Chris. I kept my answers light. They hadn't liked each other much at the beginning, particularly after Binder arrested Chris for a crime he didn't commit. Lately they'd settled into a polite but guarded relationship.

Binder already had his food and Gus hadn't spotted that I'd come in, so I got up to get my own coffee, something he tolerated. He called out for my order when I was behind the counter. "Two poached eggs, please," I responded.

"You want hash with that?"

"No thanks. Watching my figure."

Gus threw back his head and laughed. He had hawk-like features and white bushy eyebrows he used like weapons. They swooped down on you like great white birds when you said or did something he didn't like. Gus was old; nobody knew how old, but he opened his restaurant at five in the morning seven days a week for the lobstermen.

I headed back to Binder's booth. When I got there, I found that he had cleaned his plate.

"Have you followed up with any of the people who I told you about?" I asked.

He glanced at his phone to get the time. "We're talking to Willis Orsolini in fifteen minutes." So much for Will's dreams of sleeping in. "And the neighbor right after," Binder added.

"Any word on Frick's cause of death?"

Binder grinned from across the table. "I suppose there's no hope of you staying out of this?"

"You brought *me* into this. You had me picked up on the pier when I got off of work."

"You brought *you* into this. You had a meeting with the guy right before he was killed."

"Which brings me back to my question. You're admitting it was murder. Killed how?"

At that most unfortunate moment, Gus arrived. He slid my poached eggs in front of me and picked up Binder's empty plate. "Anything else?"

"Just the check," Binder answered.

"Seven oh five," Gus answered. "No time to fuss with slips of paper."

"The bean counters in the state capitol prefer documentation for expenses." Binder was too smart to take Gus on. He handed over a ten and waved Gus away when he fished in his apron for change. Gus hurried off to grab the next order.

"The cause of death," I reminded Binder. "You were going to tell me."

"I don't think I was." But then he added, "Bled to death from a puncture wound to his carotid artery."

That was news. "A puncture wound caused by what?"

Binder slid out of the booth. "I'd like to keep that under wraps for a while if we can. At least until the autopsy's official."

It wasn't until he'd disappeared up the stairs that led to the street that I remembered I'd never told him about the pile of yellowed envelopes Bart Frick had been examining at Herrickson House. And how Frick had stowed them away and slammed down the roll top on the desk when I'd entered Lou's study. It seemed like the police should at least look at them. I decided to call Binder later.

After breakfast, I headed toward Mom's house. She'd spent the night on Morrow Island with Livvie's family, her first overnight there since my father had been diagnosed with the cancer that had killed him six years earlier. It was the kind of big deal everybody tried to pretend wasn't a big deal.

Before I turned the corner onto Main Street, I spotted a familiar RV driving into town. I hadn't paid much attention to the Barnards' vehicle. I had an impression it was big and beige. As they drove past me, I noticed the giant silhouette of a lighthouse on the driver's side, and lighthouse stickers from around the US plastered across the back. Their license plate was from Arizona, which seemed a curious place for lighthouse lovers to live. Though I hadn't taken all these details in before, I was sure it was the RV I'd seen at the beach.

Glen Barnard backed the RV gingerly into an

extra-large space in the only parking lot downtown that served large RVs and tour buses. By the time I reached them, Anne had climbed out the passenger-side door, followed by Glen.

"Mr. and Mrs. Barnard, how are you? Julia Snowden. We met the day before yesterday at the beach."

"I remember," Mr. Barnard said.

"How could we forget?" Mrs. Barnard added. "Such a disappointment."

They seemed to be headed in my direction, so I walked with them. "Were you able to get your money back from Bart Frick?" I asked.

"We don't want our money back!" Anne snapped. "We want him to honor the commitment his aunt made and let us stay overnight in the keeper's cottage at Herrickson Point Light."

"We have a goal to see, touch or stay in every lighthouse in the United States," Glen explained. "Whatever access they allow, we participate at the highest level."

"Wow." There were more than sixty lighthouses in Maine alone, spread along five thousand miles of coast and islands. And this in a single state.

"We toured the west coast first," Glen explained, as if reading my mind. "It's closer to where we live. Then the Great Lakes. Now we're working our way down the east coast. Or trying to. We'd hoped to finish all, or at least most, of New England this summer and fall."

"Lighthouses light the way," Anne added. "Just as they were a beacon for sailors, they are a symbol of our hope that we will find our way safely to

shore." Her thin voice was solemn, as if weighed
down by the words. These people took their lighthouses seriously.

Did they know Frick was dead? It didn't sound
like it. On the one hand, they weren't from the
area and weren't on the local grapevine. Tourists
often traveled in happy, news-free bubbles that
were part of the experience of being on the road.
On the other hand, Jamie had said they were staying in at Camp Glooscap where Frick's murder
must be the talk of the place, just as it was everywhere else in town. And if the Barnards had hung
around the beach after I saw them barreling down
the road yesterday, they would have seen it all—
the cops, the crime scene technicians, the medical
examiner's van.

"Did you talk to Bart Frick yesterday?" I asked.

"No." Anne shook her head. "We did go down
to the beach yesterday morning to try to talk to
him. We called from the road, but he never did
come out. We couldn't figure out how to get past
the gate. That Officer Dawes climbed over that big
boulder, but we couldn't take it on. Honestly, we
don't even know if he was there."

So they didn't know. Since I'd told Binder and
Flynn the Barnards were headed toward Herrickson Point as I was leaving, the detectives would
probably be talking to them soon. I was sure they'd
prefer I didn't tell the Barnards about the murder.
They weren't friends of mine like Will was, and I
didn't feel the need to give them a heads up.

"What will you do now?" I asked.

"We'll see other lights in this area. There are historical re-enactors who give a tour of Dinkum's Light, though they're only open a couple of days a week. Gray's Light is also on an island. I'm told there are boat tours that take you past it, but you can't get off. If we really can't even get out to, much less sleep overnight at Herrickson Point Light, we'll move on down the coast. So much to see and do!"

We were in front of Mom's house. "My family's company offers an authentic Maine clambake on an island that includes a harbor tour. You can see Dinkum's, Herrickson Point and Gray's Light from our boat. We'd love to see you there while you're in the area."

Glen beamed. "Sounds wonderful."

"We'll see." Anne was much less enthusiastic. "We have a lot to do."

They moved off down the hill, both of them striding purposefully. I knew the tourist shops on Main Street would offer them more lighthouse tchotchkes than their lighthouse-loving hearts could handle.

I was almost to the steps of Mom's house when I heard a "yoo-hoo!" from across the street. "Julia! Come over and tell us about the murder," Vee Snugg called. "I have fresh raspberry muffins on the kitchen table."

CHAPTER 10

Fiona and Viola Snugg, known to all as Fee and Vee, were our dear friends and honorary great aunts. They were sisters and proprietors of the Snuggles Inn, a popular bed-and-breakfast across the street from Mom's house. When he was alive, my father had plowed their drive and shoveled their walk. Fee had planted and cared for my parents' gardens, and both sisters had looked after our empty house over the summers we'd stayed on Morrow Island.

Their kitchen was one of my favorite places in the world. As soon as I smelled Vee's raspberry muffins the resolve that had led to the poached egg breakfast evaporated. Their wooden kitchen table, dinged and dented by the loving preparation of thousands of meals, was already set for three, with china tea cups and plates painted with delicate pink flowers. I had walked into a trap.

I sat in my usual seat along the side of the table while the sisters sat at either end. Fee poured the tea. The Snuggs were in their mid-seventies and as different as sisters could be. Vee's gorgeous white hair was, as always, swept up in a chignon, her makeup perfect. Under a frilly bib apron she wore a tailored dress, hosiery, and heels, no matter the weather or the task.

Fee had worn her steel grey hair in a short pageboy for as long as I could remember. She peered at the world through thick glasses, her face clean, wrinkles unaltered. She was hunched over by painful arthritis, though it never seemed to slow her down as she stalked up and down the harbor hills with her Scottish terrier, the current one named Mackie. Neither sister had ever married.

"We heard about the trouble at Herrickson House," Vee said as she passed the muffins. "Our friend Mary Beth Gagnon has a summer cottage on Rosehill Road. She saw the officers and the medical examiner's van. They were in and out of the mansion all day. And Dan Small saw a state policeman walk you off the town pier last night. He told his mother and she told us."

"So we know you know something," Fee added. "But what do you know?"

What, indeed? I explained about how I had gone to Herrickson House, had the tour, and pleaded the case for access to the beach, with absolutely no results. And how Bart Frick was very much alive when I left. "So that's why the police wanted to talk to me," I finished.

"But how was Mr. Frick killed?" Fee blinked behind her thick glasses.

"I spoke to Lieutenant Binder at Gus's this morning. He said the autopsy isn't final." I'd lose access to the few crumbs Binder deigned to give me if he thought I was blabbing all over town.

"The lieutenant was at Gus's?" I could hear the frustration in Vee's voice. During the off-season, the sisters would have staked out the restaurant every morning until they "ran into" the lieutenant and his oh-so-handsome sergeant. In the summertime, however, they were tethered to the B&B, with guests coming and going, rooms to clean, and beds to change. Their near-daily forays to Hannaford to buy the ingredients for the English breakfasts Vee made were their only chance to get out.

"I don't think the lieutenant is staying in town," I answered. "He told me he went back to Augusta last night and returned to Busman's Harbor early this morning." I spread my arms out, palms up. "I don't know much more than you do."

"Ida Fischer's a dear friend of ours," Vee said, slathering butter on her muffin. "She goes to the Congo Church."

The Congo Church, as everyone called the Congregationalists, was one of two white-steepled churches that poked up among the other buildings that surrounded the town common. The Snugg sisters were devoted members, and regular attendees during the off-season. They couldn't attend in the summer, which they called the "re-run season," a period of recycled sermons, or visiting clergy filling in for their vacationing minister.

My mouth was full of muffin, so I nodded to show I knew of the friendship. I remembered Ida had huddled with the sisters at Lou's memorial on the *Jacquie II.*

"These last years, Lou Herrickson and Ida Fischer have been best friends more than employer–employee," Fee said. "It's a terrible time for poor Ida. To have lost her friend. And now this."

"When did Mrs. Fischer go to work for Lou?" I asked. "She's been at Herrickson House forever."

"Ida went to the Herrickson family when she was a teenager," Fee said. "It was the early sixties and the Herricksons still had a cook, a house-keeper, and a maid living in."

"That was the end of an era," Vee added. "The last gasp."

"Anyway," Fee continued the story. "Eventually Ida married and left. But later in life, many years later, she was in difficult straits and she returned to the Herricksons to beg for work. Frank and Lou were married by then and they gave her a job and a place to live. After Frank died, Ida stayed on. Her loyalty was as much to Lou at that point as it was to Frank's family."

"And to the house," Vee said. "She loves that house as if it was her own."

"And now to have that man murdered in the only home she knows." Vee shuddered.

They were silent for a moment, each lost in her own thoughts. I focused on the tangy, sweet moist-ness of Vee's raspberry muffin and waited for them to say their piece. Vee's fruit muffins were al-

ways a wonder. The muffin showcased, and never
overpowered, the fresh taste of the fruit.

"You see, the thing is—" Fee started.

"We think Ida may be in terrible trouble with
the police," Vee finished.

I'd believed the sisters were plying me with tea
and baked goods to find out what I knew about
Bartholomew Frick's murder. Now, it appeared
they had another agenda. I put the remaining corner of muffin back on my plate.

"Everyone in town knows Ida didn't think much
of Mr. Frick," Fee said.

"Two days ago, I was in an angry mob of people,
none of whom thought much of Mr. Frick," I
pointed out.

"She quit her job at Herrickson House yesterday," Vee added. "Right before the murder."

So my presence at that particular scene wasn't
yet known around town. "I don't think she should
worry." Binder and Flynn had interviewed Ida Fischer before they'd talked to me. *She* was the one
who placed *me* at the scene before Frick died, not
the other way around. "What aren't you telling
me?" I asked.

Across the table, the sisters traded glances
freighted with meaning. *How much to say?* I imagined them communicating telepathically. Fee
shook her head. "It's better if Ida tells you herself."

Vee reached across the table and took my
hands. "We think Ida is going to need your help. If
we can get her here to talk with you tomorrow
morning, will you come?"

"Of course, but I'm not sure what I can do."

"You always help people if you can." Fee seemed to have no doubt. "That's one of the many reasons we love you."

What could I say to that?

CHAPTER 11

I ran to the clambake office and confirmed I had enough commitments for steamers from my other suppliers. I had a few extra minutes, so I called Will on his cell.

"How'd it go with the police this morning?" I asked.

"About as you might expect on a day when a friend's first question is, 'How'd it go with the police?' "

"So not bad?"

"Not bad. I'm trying to stay calm. I don't want to freak Nikki out more than she already is. The cops wanted to know why my truck was at the end of Rosehill Road yesterday, so I told them. I took my boat out to clam."

But I hadn't seen him on the beach or in the water.

"I took the boat all the way around to the other side of the point," Will continued, as if sensing my doubts. "Maybe somebody saw me. I'm asking around with the lobstermen."

No wonder I hadn't seen him. "Good luck with that."

"You should try me for clams again tomorrow," he added. "The clammers on Keyport Beach have taken pity on us and we're welcome there. It's not as nice as Sea Glass, and there'll be a lot of us out there, but what Keyport lacks in charm it makes up in size. I should be able to get my full three bushels."

"That's great." I was relieved Will would be back to work. "I haven't gone clamming since my grandpa used to take Livvie and me when we were kids."

"You should come." The invitation was spontaneous.

"Really?"

"Why not? Meet me at Keyport Beach at five thirty."

Why not, indeed? It would be fun to see our food supply from harvest to plate and would give me a story to tell our guests. "You're on. See you then."

I pressed END and ran for the boat.

As the *Jacquie II* moved away from the pier, the murder of Bart Frick seemed to recede with it. The boat was full of out-of-towners, who pointed and snapped photos as Captain George told them where to look. The sky was a light, clear blue, not a cloud in sight. It was warm in town, which meant out on the water, and on Morrow Island, the temperature would be ideal.

Lunch service went off perfectly. Le Roi made his way from picnic table to picnic table, caging bits of lobster and clams from the guests who found him charming.

Emmy Bailey scurried from the kitchen to the dining pavilion, bringing the drinks, the clam chowder, and the blueberry grunt swimming in vanilla ice cream we served for dessert. I was grateful she and I didn't have time to do more than wave "hi" as we passed.

At two thirty, I rang the old ship's bell that told the guests to return to the *Jacquie II.* Captain George and his crew headed back to town and we could breathe, at least for a few minutes. Lunch was gazpacho full of summer vegetables, along with cold cuts and cheese and loaves of Italian bread. I took a bowl of the soup and sat down at a nearly empty table.

Emmy brought her bowl and sat across from me. "Did you have a chance to talk to Chris?" She asked the question before she even took a bite.

"Yes." I smiled at her to keep it light. She smiled back. "He won't be asking you about Vanessa's dad anymore."

"Thank you."

I didn't tell her that was because he'd asked me to talk to her about getting a sample of her daughter's DNA. It was way too weird. I wasn't going to ask her until and unless I knew a lot more about why Chris wanted it done, and probably not even then.

She changed the subject, describing Luther's latest, highly comic attempts at walking. We both laughed and I was relieved the Chris conversation was behind us and we were still friends.

As I finished my meal, a movement out at sea caught my eye. Quentin's racing sailboat *The Flittermouse* motored up to the side of our dock not used by the *Jacquie II*. Wyatt Jayne stood on the deck in enormous sunglasses and another selection from her apparently unlimited wardrobe of colorful summer shifts. Sonny ran to help them tie up.

The first off the boat was Quentin's new dog, Bess. Quentin had been rich since college, when he'd invented a tiny piece of code that now made every computer in the world run faster. His wealth had made him suspicious of new friends, and he'd spent most of the last twenty years moving from one lavish, lonely house to another.

Bess, a slightly overweight, middle-aged golden retriever he'd adopted from a shelter, represented a positive step in reconnecting with other living beings. Quentin's relationship with Wyatt represented another. They'd been a couple years earlier, before he'd come out. Since reconnecting, they'd fallen into a bantering friendship that benefited both of them.

Wyatt had her own stuff to deal with. Her near-engagement the previous spring had blown up spectacularly. Her almost-fiancé was still in town having his mega-yacht refitted at a local shipyard. They were talking cautiously, but nothing had come of it so far. I was glad she had Quentin's support.

I bused my bowl and met Wyatt and Quentin halfway up the lawn. "I didn't expect you two today."

"I wasn't expecting to be here, either," Wyatt said. "But I couldn't wait to share my research with you. That tip your Mom gave me about Herrickson House yielded gold." She pulled a yellowed journal from her slim leather portfolio. "Look!"

The page she held in front of me had a line drawing of the facade of Herrickson House, along with plans for the main and second floors. A label on the top of the page said, ARCHITECT: HENRY GILBERT. "Herrickson House was Gilbert's second solo commission. If Windsholme was, as I believe, his first, getting inside Herrickson House will be so illuminating, especially if the interior is relatively intact. It will tell us so much about what Gilbert intended." She looked from Quentin to me, and back again, sensing we didn't share her level of enthusiasm.

I looked over her head at him. He drew his brows together and nodded curtly. So he'd heard about the murder, or at least knew that Bart Frick was dead, which would make Wyatt's goal to see the interior of the house unlikely, if not impossible to meet in the near term. Why hadn't he told her?

"That's great, Wyatt. I, ee, er . . ." I stumbled getting the words out. "Since Mom told you about Herrickson House, there have been some complications." I glared at Quentin, willing him to help me out. He was stone-faced.

"I know the house is in an estate, if that's what

you mean. But I imagine we can get permission from the executor, or the heir . . ." she trailed off.

"That might be complicated." I told Wyatt what I knew about the situation. When I said Bart Frick had been murdered, Quentin's blonde eyebrows shot up. He hadn't heard that part.

Wyatt stopped me. "Wait. You were in the house yesterday?"

"*That's* what you got out of my story?"

"Yeah, yeah. It's really complicated. I heard you. But what about the interiors?"

I closed my eyes and remembered my tour through the rooms at Herrickson House. Bart Frick was alive and walking beside me, telling me about the paintings, the sculpture and the collections. The interior was, as I saw it, intact. Despite the profusion of art hanging on the walls, it seemed unlikely any had been moved. I hadn't seen the kitchen or any of the bathrooms, the most likely spaces to have been renovated, but Wyatt wouldn't care so much about those.

"Herrickson House is full of stuff," I told her. "But my guess is the interior hasn't been altered."

She practically bounced in her sandals.

At last, Quentin spoke up. "Since the estate is a crime scene, I don't know when we might be able to see it."

"How long can the police keep the public out?" Wyatt asked.

"It depends. Until they have what they need," I told her.

"Great," Wyatt responded. "Once they're gone,

we'll find out who inherits and we'll get permission. Who does inherit, by the way?"

Now there was a good question.

Dinner service went off without a hitch. It was a clear, warm night, perfect for folks to linger after finishing their meals, talking and drinking, while the children chased fireflies and lovers walked to the island's westernmost point to watch the sun go down in a blaze of pinks and yellows.

Clean up went quickly. Mom and I hugged Livvie and Sonny good-bye. Their kids were long in bed. Emmy Bailey put Luther in his stroller, grabbed Vanessa by the hand and we all climbed aboard the *Jacquie II* to ride home with our guests. The night sky was still clear, the stars out in profusion.

The journey back was much shorter than the one to the island. Instead of the meandering route he took out to the island to make sure our guests saw the seals and the osprey, the lighthouses, and the islands crowded with big summer homes, Captain George steered us around Westclaw Point to the entrance to the outer harbor, and then made straight for the town dock. He didn't narrate in the dark, and the crowd was quiet, full of rich food and drink.

We were never far enough out at sea to completely avoid the ambient light of the town, but the sky was still a deep black. Up above, I saw a shooting star dropping fast and straight, and then another. The Pleiades. Other people saw that one, too, and then the three that followed in quick succession. A murmur spread around the boat, the voices of children roused from near sleep, the awed tones of the adults.

About ten minutes out from the pier, my cell phone dinged quietly, downloading messages it hadn't been able to retrieve while I was on Morrow Island. I checked quickly to make sure there was nothing from Chris. If things were slow, sometimes he invited me to have a drink at Crowley's on my way home. But on a Saturday night at the height of the season, he'd be way too busy for that. None of the other messages required an immediate response. I put the phone back in my pocket.

Mom and I walked through the bustling town with Emmy and her little family. Luther was asleep, Vanessa silent. When she was at work, Emmy kept her old car in the unused third bay of Mom's garage so she didn't have to pay to park down-town. I helped her load the sleeping Luther into his car seat. Vanessa didn't say a word as she buck-led herself in beside him. She'd be asleep before they were out of town on their way to Thistle Is-land, where they lived.

After they drove off, Mom gave me a hug. "Good day today," she said.

"Good day," I agreed.

When I got home, I showered and got into my jammies. It was hot up in my top floor studio. In coastal Maine, most of us didn't have air condi-tioning. There were only three or four nights a year when we needed it. I feared this was one of them. I opened the windows in the dormers at the front and back, the big one facing the water and the small ones in the alcove that housed the bath-room. Mercifully, a breeze moved across the room.

I settled onto the couch, which faced the front window, the best place to catch the breeze. I could hear the chatter of people aboard the boats at the yacht club, the low murmur of voices, the clink of glasses.

I had a lot rumbling around in my brain. The Snugg sisters' request that I help Ida Fischer. My concerns about Will. Wyatt's question poked at me, too. Who did own Herrickson House now? Who got the art, the land, and presumably the money to sup-port it all?

Perhaps because I'd been there, possibly the last person to see Bart Frick alive except for his killer, I'd thought of the events of the last few days as the trigger for the murder, and the people around me as suspects.

But Bart Frick must have done something be-fore he arrived in Busman's Harbor. A man in his forties, by the look of him. Did he have a family? He'd been living at Herrickson House alone, but maybe he had a wife and kids who were coming later?

I opened my laptop and typed "Bartholomew Frick" into a search engine. Fortunately, it was an unusual name. All the first hits were stories about his murder. It had been covered locally, of course, as well as in the big Maine papers and the *Boston Globe.* The articles told me nothing new.

I found his website easily. Frick had once worked for a large insurance company, but his website now said he was a consultant. I didn't understand what the description said he did. It was somehow related to figuring out how to insure ship cargo. There was no list of clients on his site. My old boss had said, "Unemployed blue-collar guys are contractors, unemployed white-collar guys are consultants." I wondered how robust Frick's consulting business had actually been. The "About" section of the site was plain vanilla, nothing personal.

Extrapolating from the date of his undergraduate degree confirmed my impression he was in his forties. Further searching showed he lived in a big apartment building in Brookline, Massachusetts. I couldn't tell if he owned or rented. I wondered if he'd had the red Porsche all along, or if it was new since he'd become the "Responsible Person," for Lou's estate.

I tried "Bart Frick," and didn't get much more, a few registrations for charity road races around Boston and on Cape Cod. A search for other Fricks in Brookline didn't turn up a wife, though perhaps she'd kept her own name. But that wasn't the impression I got as I read. He had no business partners, no siblings. No family I could find, except for Lou, of course. It seemed Bart Frick was profoundly alone.

He must have a will. Presumably, he had assets of his own, not only what he'd inherited from his great-uncle's wife. Was he planning to live in Herrickson House, at least seasonally? It seemed more likely he planned to tear it down and develop the land. Then it made more sense for him to block the access road. He was trying to prove the property had exclusive rights to the beach and lighthouse.

Which brought me back to Busman's Harbor. How many people would be infuriated if the beach and lighthouse became private, if Herrickson House was torn down and the land divided into prime oceanfront lots? Many people. Thousands. But who among them would be infuriated enough to kill?

I felt the computer slipping from my lap. My eyes flew open and I grabbed it before it fell to the floor. I hadn't realized I'd fallen asleep. I gave up and went to bed. I didn't wake up when Chris came home.

CHAPTER 12

My phone clanged an alarm at four thirty the next morning. For a heart-pounding moment, I thought it was an emergency call waking me in the dark. Then I realized I'd committed to go clamming with Will. I slipped out of bed and into a pair of cutoffs, and an old Snowden Family Clambake T-shirt. I threw a tube of sunblock and a Red Sox cap into my tote bag, put on a pair of flip-flops and was on my way. Chris didn't move the whole time.

Keyport Beach was at the end of Eastclaw Point, farther away than Sea Glass and in the opposite direction. I stopped at the gas station mini-mart for coffee and a banana. The sun was a thin, bright orange line in the east.

By the time I parked in the lot at Keyport Beach, the sun was up, a diffuse light across the landscape. Will's dark red pickup was there, along with several others. I got out of my car and slathered on the sunblock. The tide was near dead low and the

salty smell of the Atlantic Ocean woke me up better than the coffee.

The clammers were spread out, working near
the tide line as the water moved out. I spotted Will
about midway down the beach and called to him.
Unlike other forms of hunting, the clams couldn't
hear you and run away. Will didn't hear me over
the sounds of breaking waves and screaming gulls.
He didn't turn around.

When I reached him, he greeted me with a
smile. "Glad you came."

"Thanks for asking me."

"You've done this before?"

"Years ago, with my grandpa. He used to take us
for quahogs."

"Hard shells," he responded. "Maybe we'll try to
get some later when the tide comes in. But mainly
we're looking for soft shells—steamers."

I nodded to show I understood. He handed me
a clam rake, the short-handled fork with the bent
tines and basket he and the other clammers had
raised at Bart Frick's gate. "Won't you need this?" I
asked.

"No. It's Nikki's. I'll use my shovel." He pulled a
rusty spade with a worn wooden handle from the
sand.

The clam rake he'd given me was shiny and new.
Nikki must not go clamming frequently. I was sure
Will had raised a rusty, well-used clam rake at the
gate at Herrickson Point.

"It's about twenty minutes to low," Will said.
"We'll follow the tide out and then back in again."
He put the spade over his shoulder, picked up a

large galvanized bucket half-filled with seawater, and walked on the hard sand. He wore rubber boots as well as rolled-up jeans and a white T-shirt. "Do you know what you're looking for?"

I tried to remember. "Bubbles?"

"Holes," he answered. "Here I'll show you." In about ten feet he stopped. I stared at the sand, seeing nothing. With a big gesture, he shoved the spade into the sand. Immediately a dozen or more tiny holes appeared. "We scared 'em," Will said. "They contract and push out the water that creates the holes."

"How did you know where they were?"

He shrugged. "I just do. You learn to read the sand if you do this enough." He caught my skeptical look. "Don't worry. A lot of times the holes will already be there." He took the spade and dug a shallow hole about six inches from the mini-dots in the sand. When it was eight or nine inches around, clamshells began to show at the edge of the bowl. Will stuck the shovel into the sand and dropped to his haunches over the hole. He reached in, quickly grabbing clam after clam and sliding them into the galvanized bucket. "Get in there," he urged.

I squatted across the hole from him, plunged my hand into the cool water and touched a clamshell. "Where'd it go?" I'd had a finger on one, but it had disappeared.

"Soft shells can only move vertically," Will said without pausing at his work. "You alarmed him and he scooted. Keep at least a finger on it so you can track it going down. Try again."

I reached into the hole again. There were three

shells still visible. This time, I kept my index finger on the shell as it moved down through the wet sand with surprising speed. "Got you!" I pulled him out and dumped him into Will's bucket.

When the hole was empty, Will stood up and we moved down the beach a little. "The tide seems like it's barely moved," I said.

"Tide moves the least in the twenty minutes before and after the low," Will responded. "Here."

This time there were holes visible on the surface before he tapped the shovel on the sand. Will repeated his process, digging down next to the little holes, waiting until the bowl filled with water and digging the clams out with his hands. There weren't nearly so many in this colony, seven total, but I managed to retrieve three of them.

"Foraging for bivalves was probably the earliest form of humans hunting," Will said as we worked. "No equipment or skill required. Well, maybe a rock to open the shells."

"Seems like a skill to me." I watched his hands as, lightning fast, he pulled the last clam out of the water. I knew prehistoric man ate lots of clams and other shellfish. The middens, or mounds of shells, were still occasionally visible on riverbanks just inland.

Up and down the beach, I could see about a dozen other people close to the water line, digging and bending, straightening up, and moving their heavy pails. Most were men, but there were a couple of women.

"It's crowded," Will said, following my gaze. "That's why I don't usually come here. About half these folks are regulars. Truth is, they're being nice about the rest of us clamming here because we can't get onto Sea Glass. We stay out of each other's way."

I was used to that sort of thing, people marking out a territory on land or water they didn't own. Lobstermen did it in the harbor and along the coast. The people who fished for baby eels, called elvers, did it along riverbanks in the spring. Keyport Beach belonged to an association of cottages that lay over a line of boulders and across Eastclaw Point Road. They'd always tolerated or even encouraged clammers, dog walkers, surf casters, and others as long as people cleaned up after themselves and avoided prime beach hours.

"Your turn," Will said.

"Here." I indicated a circle of sand about a foot in circumference with lots of the tiny holes close together.

"They're probably too small," he said. "But give it a go."

I used the claw-like tines of the rake to move the sand, creating a bowl that filled halfway with water about six inches from the tiny holes. Then I squatted and worked the sides of the bowl with my hands.

The first clam got away from me. I got a hold of the second and pulled him out. Will was right. The shell was less than an inch from the hinge to the outside curve. To make sure, I pulled out another. Same thing.

"How did you know they'd be too small?"

"Holes were too close together."

I picked up the rake and we walked a little farther. The tide had turned, and was coming in. "Here?" I asked, indicating a few dots in the sand.

Will shook his head. "Naw. Someone's been there before us." He pointed with his shovel to a small mound of sand, nearly washed away with the tide, the remnants of someone else's digging as the tide went out. "Keep looking."

"How many months do you clam?" The Snowden Family Clambake bought steamers from Father's Day to Columbus Day. The rest of the year we were shut down.

"Now, all year round."

Clamming was legal all twelve months in Maine. It was hard work all the time, but especially miserable and dangerous in the winter. The question had been my way of asking Will what other kinds of work he did. No one in Busman's Harbor, as far as I knew, made a living entirely from clamming. It was a good supplement to something else, or multiple something elses. The word "now" in Will's answer told me there was more to the story. I waited to see if he'd explain.

"I started off as a commercial fisherman, when I was just out of school. Leave it to me to pick something there was no future in."

Busman's Harbor had once had a thriving fishing fleet, but a poorly understood combination of over-fishing, foreign competition, and a warming ocean had decimated the fishing grounds of the North Atlantic. One by one, the boats had disappeared from the harbor until there were none.

"I shrimped in the winter," Will said.

Catching the delicious, tiny Gulf of Maine shrimp had been lucrative winter fishery for Maine lobstermen and others. The season had run from December through February for many years, but there had been no season at all for the last five. With the catch down dramatically, the state had called it off, creating another hardship for fishermen. I loved the tiny, sweet shrimp and missed them in the summertime, fried and served in a basket with French fries and coleslaw.

Will stopped at the next set of holes we came to and dug with his shovel, talking as he worked. "For a while, I had a winter gig doing security at the oceanographic lab, but it didn't work out. Nikki's mom watches the kids so she can work at Kidder's Department Store four days a week during the season." Kidder's was right off the town pier, a jumble of Maine-y souvenirs. Will dropped to his haunches and plunged his hand into the cold water in the hole. "Nikki's worried all the time. It's been hard. I won't lie. The Snowden Family Clambake being a regular customer has been a godsend."

It was a sadly familiar story in a place where seasonal work dominated. I hadn't realized things were so tough for Will and his family.

We spread out and each worked on our own. Will returned to his truck a few times to get another pail. Maine clammers were allowed to take three bushels a day. A bushel of soft shells weighs fifty pounds, so Will used pails that held smaller quantities to make them easier to carry. The work was backbreaking. As the sun rose, Will took off his shirt, revealing heavily muscled chest and arms. I put more sunblock on the back of my neck.

When the third pail was full, Will stood up, stretching his back. "Time to go." The beach was empty. I hadn't noticed when the other clammers had taken off.

As we gathered our equipment, a Busman's Harbor PD patrol car pulled into the parking lot, which was empty except for my Caprice and Will's truck.

"Did you go to town hall and get that shellfish license I told you about?" Will asked.

My stomach dropped. "You didn't tell me to—" I stopped. Will was grinning, obviously kidding. But I should have known to get a day license.

The patrol car stopped and Jamie Dawes got out, swinging his long legs to the ground as he pulled on his cap. "Hey, Will," he said as we approached.

"Hey, Jamie."

"Lieutenant Binder and Sergeant Flynn want to interview you again."

"That so." Will hefted the big pail into the back of his pickup. The water sloshed out, hitting him in the chest.

"And they'd like you to bring your equipment with you," Jamie said. "Voluntarily."

"Why would that be?"

"We're talking to all the people who protested at Frick's gate on Thursday, and we're looking at everybody's equipment, if they're willing."

"You should talk to a lawyer," I told Will. "This is

the second time they've questioned you. You don't have to turn over your equipment."

Up to this point, they'd both ignored me. The conversation, the tension, was between them.

Will turned to me. "I can't afford a lawyer. Don't need one anyway." He turned back to Jamie. "I'll come. Can I stop at my house and get cleaned up?"

"We're on a tight schedule." Jamie kept his voice even, all business, though he'd told me dealing as a cop with townspeople he knew well was one of the toughest parts of his job.

"Okay. I'll be right behind you."

Jamie got in the patrol car and Will in his truck. They both pulled out of the lot in a cloud of sand and dust. I watched them go.

Lieutenant Binder had said Bart Frick had bled out from a puncture wound in his carotid artery. Now the detectives were looking at the equipment of everyone who'd gathered at the gate across the beach. They must suspect the hole had been made by a clam rake, or something like it.

I stood in the deserted parking lot, worrying about Will, and Nikki and their kids, and wondering what had happened to Will's old clam rake.

CHAPTER 13

We'd started clamming so early it was eight o'clock, my usual start-work time, when I pulled the Caprice into Mom's garage. I gave Mom a wave as I walked by, headed for the back stairs. I went up to my office and did the normal stuff, ordering food and supplies, finding coverage for an employee who'd called in sick. She was a college sophomore on her third case of "Morning-after-Saturday-nights," which meant she wouldn't be coming back next year. I checked in with our ticket kiosk on the town pier. We were sold out for both lunch and dinner.

I finished up, called good-bye to Mom, and headed out the front door. If I kept moving, I could get back to my apartment, grab a quick shower, and change before I had to meet the boat. I was down the walk when I heard a familiar, "Yoo-hoo!" Vee Snugg stood in her high heels on the porch of the Snuggles Inn, waving madly. I crossed the street. "Good morning, Julia. What a surprise to see you."

"Really? Because I come out of Mom's house this time pretty much every day." I wrinkled my nose at her. What was she up to?

"Since you're passing by, would you like to come in for tea and sour cream coffee cake?"

"Passing? I'm not passing, I'm on my way to my apartment. Why are you shouting?"

Standing above me on the porch, Vee shook me off with a quick gyration of her head. "We thought, since you're passing by, you might like to come in," she repeated at the same volume. "We have another visitor, Ida Fischer. Perhaps you know her?"

Light dawned. Ida hadn't so much agreed to meet with me as been tricked into it. "I'd be delighted to see her."

Vee rolled her eyes. "About time," she muttered. Then louder, "Come in, come in."

Mackie ran to greet me when I entered. I bent down and scratched him behind the ears. As Vee passed through the swinging door to the kitchen, I caught a glimpse of Ida Fischer slumped in a chair at the table. "Julia Snowden's just dropped by," Vee announced. "From across the street."

I followed Vee. "I can only stay a minute or two. I've got to get dressed for work."

Fee looked at me, taking in my denim cutoffs, faded Snowden Family Clambake T-shirt, and flip-flops, and said, "Indeed. Do you know each other?"

"We met the other day," I answered.

Ida Fischer fixed me with an unwavering stare. "We did. I had no idea that it would be the last time either of us saw poor Mr. Frick."

Poor Mr. Frick? That was rich. Ida had said she couldn't stand him. And, was I mistaken, or did Ida go out of her way to say "the last time *we* saw him." I knew it was the last time *I'd* seen Frick, but I couldn't vouch for her.

I sat at the table. Fee poured tea while Vee divided the coffee cake left over from their guests' breakfast. I was starving after my exertions of the morning. I accepted my piece gratefully. Like everything Vee baked, the coffee cake was delicious, a mouthwatering combination of sour and sweet.

"We're so sorry for your trouble," Fee told Ida. "First Lou, and then this . . ."

"And my job. It's been a bad run." Ida paused while she gathered herself. "Lou was over a hundred. I knew I'd lose her sometime, unless I went first. I miss her terribly, but I was prepared. But a murder in Herrickson House, my home for all these years?" She shuddered. "That takes all."

Fee and Vee made sympathetic noises.

"The police won't let me get my things. Not that I want to go in there."

"Remind me, how long have you lived at Herrickson House?" Vee asked.

Ida's angular face squeezed in on itself with concentration. "The first time, I was there for three years." She turned to me, "I was a maid for Mrs. Herrickson, the late Mr. Herrickson's mother, back in the days when they kept a full staff in the summer. Since I returned, I've been there more than thirty years."

"Where were the Herricksons from?" I asked

"Why here, of course. I'm surprised, a local girl like you wouldn't know that."

"I know Herrickson Point Light is named for them, and they have an ancestor who was the keeper."

Vee nodded. "Cyrus Herrickson. He bought the land from the road to the point so when his job at the lighthouse ended he wouldn't have to leave."

"Did he build Herrickson House?" If Ida knew something about the history of the house, Wyatt Jayne would be thrilled.

"No, no," Ida answered. "The money came later, from manufacturing shoes."

That was news to me, but at one time over half the shoes sold in the United States were made in New England, so it made sense.

"They had a place about a hundred miles inland in the town where their factory was," Ida continued. "The house on Herrickson Point was built in the 1890s I think. When I was in service, old Mrs. Herrickson came here with her daughter and grandchildren for the summer, every year without fail. The men, old Mr. Herrickson, Francis, who later became Lou's husband, and Mr. Frick who was married to the daughter, came for the weekends."

"The daughter was Bart Frick's grandmother." I remembered what he'd told me during our first and last conversation.

"He was the grandnephew of Francis, yes," Ida affirmed. "He inherited it all. Lou thought he should, since the land and house came from the Herrickson side. I just wish he'd been a nicer person."

"The money, however, came from Lou," Vee put in.

I raised an eyebrow at her. This was new information.

"The shoe company fell on hard times," she explained. "As they all did. First, they moved the factory to the South, and then abroad, but they couldn't hang on. The famous Herrickson Moccasin brand disappeared. Francis was the only one left at that point. He'd left the family business to practice law in Portland. He sold the big house in western Maine for pennies on the dollar and moved to Busman's Harbor full-time. He still had a lot of wealthy friends though. After his mother died and he gave up his law practice, he was visiting a friend in Palm Beach when he met Heloise Jameson."

"Where did Lou's money come from?" I asked.

"Her parents. It was mining money. Pennsylvania," Fee answered.

"And she'd married well," Vee added. "A few times before she met Francis."

"She was nearly fifty when they married," Ida took up the tale. "When he brought her here, after a whirlwind courtship, no one thought it would last. He'd never been married. Hard for a leopard to change its spots at sixty years of age. Herrickson House is beautiful, of course, but Busman's Harbor isn't Palm Beach. But she threw herself into the community. Gave to every charity, belonged to every service organization. She loved the town and it loved her back.

"They kept the house in Palm Beach and spent the winters there until Frank passed away twenty-five years ago. By then Lou was getting on, and moving back and forth every year was too much. She had to choose one place or the other. Everyone thought she would choose Florida. Everyone except me. I knew how much she loved that place."

"So there were no other heirs, besides Bart Frick?" The question of Bart's will and what would happen now was pinging around my brain.

"He was the only one left," Ida sighed. "And now he's gone. They're all gone."

"It's interesting that you returned to your old job after so much time away," I said.

"When I left Herrickson House the first time, I married and left town with my husband. He turned out to be, well, not a nice man. When I came back to town many years later, I was desperate. I was in my forties, with no skills and not much education, living with my sister whose house was already overflowing with her husband and five kids. Lou heard about me from my sister's husband's cousin who did some carpentry for her. She told Francis, 'If she was here before, we must have her back.' I don't think he agreed, but he loved her so much, he would do anything she asked.

"So I moved into Herrickson House for the second time. I was the only live-in staff by then. Gardeners and cleaners came and went, but otherwise it was me. When Frank was alive, I watched over the place while he and Lou were in Palm Beach. You'd think it would get lonely out there on the point. All the other houses on the road were closed up for the winter. But I loved it."

"Who will inherit now?" I asked.

"I don't know. I hope, whoever it is, they will leave the house as it is. That's what Lou wanted."

We were silent for a moment after that. I felt badly for Ida, who had lost her job and her home. My previous suspicion of her felt silly.

"Did Lou . . . take care of you?" Fee asked softly. A blush rose to her already ruddy cheeks. Mainers rarely asked others about money.

"She did," Ida answered. "I'll be okay. I won't live out my life at Herrickson House, as I'd hoped, but I wouldn't have even if Mr. Frick were still alive. We didn't get on, as you saw, Julia. I am sorry for my outburst the other day."

She'd dropped the pretense of "poor Mr. Frick," and was being more honest. Now we were getting somewhere. "No need to apologize," I said. "You've been through a lot."

"It's just that," she clenched her fists on the table, "when someone disrespects Lou, or Herrickson House, I get so mad. It's my home, or it was, and that kind woman took me in when no one else would give me a chance."

"Ida, did you know Julia has helped several people in town who've run into trouble with the police?" Vee asked. The question felt out-of-the-blue, though I knew what the sisters were up to.

Ida squinted her blue eyes at me, obviously re-assessing. "I didn't know that," she answered, a note of caution in her voice.

"She has," Fee said, "and Vee and I thought, per-haps, Julia could help you, too. If you think you might need help, that is."

Mrs. Fischer drew her brows together, taking in what they'd said. She nodded, not rejecting the offer, but not accepting it, either. The three of us waited, looking at her.

"I doubt you need any help," I told her. "The state police know you left the house before Bart Frick was murdered. You didn't like him, but not many did. I don't think there's cause for alarm."

Another silence followed, heavier than the last. Mrs. Fischer broke it. "My dear friends think I have cause for concern because they know something about me you don't. I killed my husband, you see. For most of the years I was away from Herrickson House, I was in prison."

My astonished reaction was unfortunately obvi-ous to all of them. I consciously closed my gaping mouth, giving Mrs. Fischer a tight grin.

"So if you could help me, dear, I would appreci-ate it," she said. "When a crime is committed, the police love to look no further than at the crimi-nals."

From the harbor came the three familiar deep calls of the *Jacquie II*. Ten minutes to the boat. There'd be no time for a shower now. I jumped up from the table, nearly knocking over my chair, and thanked the ladies for the tea and cake.

Vee walked me to the door. "You'll help Ida, won't you?"

"Of course," I said, "but she'll have to tell me everything. The whole story."

"I'll tell her," Vee said.

CHAPTER 14

Mom was coming out of her house as I ran out of the Snuggles Inn. "Ready for work?" She looked me up and down—salt splattered cutoffs, T-shirt, flip-flops and all. She didn't have to say anything.

"Maybe Livvie has something I can wear."

Mom nodded curtly. Between my sister's tall, broad-shouldered swimmer's body and my petite size, we hadn't been able to share clothes for a decade and a half.

We passed the police station as we fast walked toward the town pier. The parking lot was full of pickup trucks. The clammers who'd protested at Herrickson Point bringing their clam rakes in for voluntary inspection, no doubt.

The double glass doors of the building opened and Jamie walked out with Glen and Anne Barnard. He shook hands with each of them, taking his time, looking each in the eye and saying something before he let the hand go. They came across the parking lot toward Mom and me.

"We're headed the same way you are," Glen said when they reached us. "We have tickets for your lunchtime boat." Glen was smiling, but Anne looked mad or sad, I couldn't tell which. She wore a knitted sweater vest with a lighthouse blazing up one side of it. Glen's navy pants were covered in tiny red and white lighthouses. I introduced them both to Mom.

"We'd better keep moving," Mom said. "The whistle has already sounded."

Once we were on the *Jacquie II*, I forgot to be self-conscious about what I was wearing. The day was gorgeous and the crowd, clustered in family groups, was excited. There were more children than usual, and while the adults were always appreciative of the seals, the kids were even more enthusiastic, crowing and cheering as Captain George pointed them out.

"Look, Mom, a sea gull!" A little girl pointed toward the bow, awestruck. Her happiness made me smile. Normally we call the pesky birds "dump gulls," because there always seemed to be more of them at the dump than on the water.

I found the Barnards on the open top deck. "There are great views of all three lighthouses on this trip," I told them. "We'll pass Dinkum's first, which is on a harbor island. Then Herrickson Point Light, which you know. We'll see it from the water, looking across Sea Glass Beach. The third one is Gray's Light, which you'll see from the distance when we're almost to Morrow Island."

"Thanks," Glen said. "And thank you for recommending your clambake to us. We're making the best of a bad situation."

"It's not the same as staying overnight at the keeper's cottage," Anne complained.

"But still—" her husband chided.

Over the ship's sound system, Captain George pointed out Dinkum's Light just ahead.

Anne rallied, clapping her hands. "First lighthouse in the State of Maine."

"A technicality," Glen added. "Maine didn't become a state until the Missouri Compromise of 1820. Until then it was a colony of Massachusetts. Dinkum's was built in 1821, thus the first light in the new state, but not the oldest along the Maine coast by any means."

"I'll give you a heads up when we get in sight of Herrickson Point," I said. "That won't be until we're through the mouth of the harbor."

They thanked me and I went to the pilothouse. Captain George was in a fine mood, like everyone else on board. He'd worked for my father, and then for my brother-in-law Sonny when he ran the clambake, and now, technically, he worked for me. But I didn't fool myself I was in any way his boss. He knew more about the harbor, the *Jacquie II*, and the crew than anyone. I couldn't imagine a situation in which I would second-guess him.

I was surprised to find my mother on the bridge along with George. Since she'd come back to work at the clambake in the spring, she normally sat on the lower deck and read a book, treating the boat ride like a daily commute. I raised an eyebrow at her, a signal she either didn't see or chose to ignore.

"What a beautiful day!" I said.

"That it is," George confirmed. "Enjoy it while it's here. Rough weather tomorrow."

One of the many things I *always* did was check the weather forecast, but I hadn't done it that morning.

"They're expecting a blow," George added.

"George thinks we'll be closed tomorrow," Mom told me.

I looked at George, who nodded yes. He knew having the clambake up and running every day of the summer was important to us financially. He wouldn't have even considered closing unless conditions were going to be dangerous.

I pulled out my cell. "Let me see if I can reach the ticket kiosk before we leave the harbor. At least I can tell them to stop taking reservations for tomorrow."

But it was too late. I had no reception. The *Jacquie II* slipped out of the harbor's mouth and turned west toward Morrow Island. I excused myself to go back to the Barnards.

They were still where I'd left them, smiling broadly.

"Herrickson Point will be visible right . . . there." I pointed as the lighthouse came into sight.

"It's even more beautiful from the water than it is from the land," Glen said.

He was right. Because the lighthouse sat on a rocky ledge at the far point of the beach, from the land it looked protected. But from the water it looked thrust out of the rocks, on its own. At high tide, which it was, the sliver of sand that led to its rocky perch was all but invisible from the water. The lighthouse and rocks looked like they were about to float out to sea.

Herrickson Point Light was a beautiful building, forty feet tall, painted white with a distinctive red strip about a third of the way from the top. The keeper's house was also white, and small, only four rooms. It snuggled next to the light tower on the small outcropping.

Captain George slowed down so people could enjoy the view and take lots of photos. I stared across the water. There wasn't a soul in the parking lot, by the lighthouse, or up at the mansion. All wrong for a gorgeous summer day.

"They say the keeper's house is haunted," I told the Barnards.

"We know the story," Anne replied. Of course they did. "One day in the winter of 1901," she said, "the keeper hiked from the light over to Westclaw Village to collect his mail. The village in those days had a post office, general store, and Baptist Church."

"As it does today," I said.

"We stopped in the village," Anne said. "So charming. On his way, the keeper saw a woman, alone, walking toward the point. Except for the keeper, all the year-rounders lived in the village. He called out to her to see if she was lost."

Anne stopped to take a breath. I was enjoying her telling of the familiar tale. "The next day her body, weighed down by stones in the pockets of her coat, washed up on Sea Glass Beach. Her clothes were expensive. She must have been a woman of means."

"The local people were convinced she must have been a summer person, or a guest," Glen finished. "Otherwise how would she have known about the beach? But no one ever came looking for her."

"They say she's still there," I told them. I was only half kidding. "They" did say it, all the time. "In the daylight, she can be seen from the keeper's cottage, swimming in the surf in her turn-of-the-century clothes. And night she walks through the rooms."

"Do you think it's true?" Anne asked.

"The story? Yes," I answered. "Unlike most of the 'legends' you'll hear around here, it is. She's buried in the Herrickson family plot in the little Westclaw Village cemetery. Her headstone says UNKNOWN MERMAID, because she returned to the sea."

"I meant, do you think the ghost part is true?" Anne said. "I hoped to see her when we stayed in the keeper's cottage."

I started to say, no, I didn't believe in ghosts, but Anne's expression was so sad it stopped me. "I don't know. I don't think anyone does," I answered.

"Now, honey. We may not be able to stay at the lighthouse, but we're making the best of our time here," Glen reminded her.

"We will stay there," Anne insisted "We'll stay there before we leave."

I didn't think they would, but I didn't say so.

Anne seemed so bent on it. I wondered about this strange couple and their fanatical dedication to their lighthouse quest. What motivated them? And why did not getting this single notch on their belts, the overnight at the keeper's cottage at Herrickson Point Light, make Anne so melancholy?

I told the Barnards where to look on the horizon for Gray's Light and left them. The tour was almost over.

As Morrow Island came into view, the crowd on the boat came alive again, chattering and pointing across the water. The enormous bonfire that would heat the rocks Sonny would use to cook the lobsters and steamers was visible on the shore.

Once I'd done my bit helping everyone ashore, I went to the kitchen to find Livvie and beg for a change of clothes. Fortunately, she did have something I could wear, a shapeless black shift. It hit her above the knees, but fell on me to mid-calf. The top swam on me, but it was better than the cutoffs.

After I changed, I walked back to the dining pavilion from Livvie's cottage, watching the many kids who'd been on the boat—playing volleyball on the great lawn, running up the hill toward the beach, discovering the playhouse in the woods that was a perfect miniature of Windsholme.

Lately, in moments that took me by surprise, I'd been tearing up at the sight of infants and toddlers. I'd started imagining a baby with a dimple in her chin and bright green eyes. I hadn't said anything about it to Chris. We talked about the future all the time. We talked about Christmas and vacations. We planned to run our dinner restaurant, Gus's Too, again in the off-season. Sometimes Chris even talked about things further out, like when he could stop renting his lakeside cabin during tourist season and we could move there permanently.

His cabin had three bedrooms. In my vision of the future I saw a crib in one of them. But we hadn't talked about children. Or marriage. I could talk to Chris about anything, with three exceptions, his family, weddings, and babies. The mention of any one of them, even in casual conversation, shut him down.

I went to check on Mom in the gift shop and ran into the Barnards inspecting the wares. From behind them, I pointed to the sturdy green mugs up on a high shelf, engraved with the images of the three Busman's Harbor lighthouses. Mom, catching my movement, nodded silently and pulled two down for their inspection.

"Perfect," Glen said. "A souvenir of our time in Busman's Harbor. It hasn't been what we expected, but it hasn't been uninteresting, either." He pulled out his wallet.

When the Barnards left, Mom and I were alone in the shop. "Did you ever hear that Ida Fischer murdered her husband?" I asked.

"Goodness, Julia. Where did that come from?" She looked at me. "Never mind. I know. This Frick business has brought it all up again."

"So you did know, about Mrs. Fischer I mean?"

Mom's brow furrowed. "It happened a long time

ago, when I was a girl. I didn't hear about it then, but when Ida came back to town and went to work at Herrickson House, the talk came back."

"What was the talk?"

"She murdered her husband and spent twenty years at the Women's Correctional Center."

"Twenty years!"

"It could have been life." Maine hadn't had a death penalty since 1885.

"Do you know how she did it?"

Mom spread her hands on the counter. "Only rumors. You know how people talk."

"What did people say?"

"They said she beat him to death with a clam rake." She paused. "Julia, are you okay? You're white as a sheet."

I did feel a little woozy. I thought of the police, checking all those clam rakes. Did they know about Ida's past? They must. "I'm fine," I said. But I wasn't.

Dinner was as busy as lunch. I ran from guest to guest, making sure their glasses were full and so were their tummies, but I had trouble focusing. I believed Bart Frick had been killed with a clam rake. Ida Fischer was rumored to have killed her husband with a clam rake. Will Orsolini was missing a clam rake. These thoughts tumbled around and around in my head like socks in a dryer. I didn't want Ida to be the murderer. I didn't want Will to be.

There had to be some other answer.

By the end of dinner service the weather had turned. Low clouds drifted westward rapidly, pausing only to give us a glorious sunset. By the time we loaded the last of the guests and staff of the *Jacquie II*, the wind had come up as well. It was still more a breeze than a blow, but enough of one to tell us a change was coming.

"Why don't you come to my house," Mom said to Livvie before we boarded. "Spend a rainy day in town. I'm sure you have plenty of errands you could get done."

A sleeping Jack curled against Livvie's shoulder. "We're all exhausted. We can all use a quiet day right here."

Mom had stayed on the island with us when we were babies. Livvie was determined to do the same.

I was the last person to board the boat. "Rain's coming for sure," Captain George said. "No clambake tomorrow."

CHAPTER 15

I woke the next morning to the sound of wind-driven rain pounding on the big, harbor-facing window in the studio. Chris stirred beside me. The rain meant a light day for him, too, his landscaping work postponed. Later in the day, he would take his cab out and give rides to tourists who preferred not to get wet, but first there was time to enjoy a cozy, slow start to the morning.

It was nine by the time we showered and dressed. "Pancakes?" Chris asked, pointing to the floor.

I smiled at him. "Of course!" My nose had been attuned to the smells coming from Gus's place all morning.

Gus's was mobbed and noisy, full of lobstermen and tour boat operators, ferry crews, and pleasure sailors. The retail workers still had to report for duty, but everyone who worked on the water had the summer equivalent of a snow day. Just as with a snow day, they were happy for the break, as long as it didn't last too long.

Slickers hung on the back of every chair. Chris started for two open stools at the counter, but I held him back. Much as I didn't want to bring our idyllic morning to a close, we had to talk. He squinted, bringing his light brown brows together over those green eyes, but moved to the line for a booth.

Time passed slowly. No one was in a hurry to go back out into the storm. Chris shifted from one foot to the other, looking pointedly at the two counter places, which were now occupied. Then, as if a bell had sounded, five groups got up at once, shuffling into their rain gear, and the rest of us made a beeline for the empty booths.

I put my Snowden Family tote on the red faux-leather banquette cushion, then went behind the counter, and grabbed a tub to bus the tables. Because Chris and I operated a dinner restaurant in his space during the off-season, Gus tolerated us helping out, even if we never, ever did anything quite to his exacting standards.

I put the dirty dishes in the tub and wiped the tables down. Then I took the dishes back to the kitchen and deposited them by the old conveyor-belt-style dishwasher. As he did every summer, Gus had hired a local kid to work in the back. Gus always picked the last kid anyone else would hire, a young person down on his luck with financial or family troubles, or both, since the two so often came together.

This year's version was Kyle. He was nowhere to be seen, but a whiff of tobacco smoke came through the screen on the kitchen door, telling me where he was.

"Kyle! Dishes piling up in here."

"Coming."

By the time I got back, Chris was settled in the booth, his long legs under the table. Gus approached and took our order: coffees, blueberry pancakes, and bacon, a rainy day treat. The blueberries would be fresh this time of year and not frozen, which made them extra special, and drowned in Maine-made maple syrup, the only kind Gus carried.

Gus brought the coffee on his return trip and disappeared again. There was no putting it off any longer, but how to start the conversation? I'd gotten nowhere up until then; what would make this time different?

As luck would have it, I didn't have to start. Chris did. "Did you talk to Emmy yet? About the DNA test, I mean."

"No."

"Too busy?"

I could have taken the easy way out. The day before had been busy, and I'd been distracted, but I didn't. "No. Not too busy. Chris," I put my elbows on the table and leaned toward him, lowering my voice. "I'm not comfortable asking Emmy until I know what this is really about."

"What do you mean? You know what it's about. I want to know if Vanessa is my niece."

I settled back into the seat and deliberately let my arms fall loosely at my sides, signaling that I was open to understanding, open to listening. "All due respect, honey, is that really your business? Emmy doesn't want to know. Your brother doesn't want to know. Emmy hasn't indicated Vanessa has started asking questions. She sees Emmy's ex as her father. Your brother's in prison. He has nothing to offer her. Why aren't you willing to wait, and let the adults in this situation sort it out? If they ever do."

Gus chose that not particularly great moment to put our plates down in front of us. The smell of the pancakes wafted toward me, softening me up. Chris looked at his plate longingly, like he wanted to dive in and let the rest of the conversation drift away. But, to his credit, he didn't. He squared his shoulders and looked me in the eye.

"I've never talked to you about my family. I know that's been hard for you."

I nodded to show I'd heard.

"My mother is sick. Very sick. And it's genetic."

The booth began to tilt. "What kind of . . . ?"

"Huntington's. She has Huntington's disease." His familiar voice was thick with emotion.

The melted butter began to congeal on top of the cooling pancakes. Huntington's Disease. The little bit I knew about it was enough to terrify me. Woody Guthrie's disease. Paralysis. Dementia. Early death. Passed from parent to child. The picture I'd had in my head of the baby with the dimple and green eyes disappeared with a pop like a balloon. Tears sprang behind my eyes. "But she's alive?" I asked.

He nodded. I wasn't sure he could speak.

"But you never go to see her." Despite my efforts my voice rose. Someone in the booth behind us turned to look. I'd often urged Chris to visit his parents during the off-season. Last winter, he'd traveled to Florida, not the part where his parents lived, but still, he'd passed so much closer than we were here, yet he hadn't gone to see them.

My heart ached. Chris had a loving heart. I was certain of it, but he never visited his mother, who was sick, who was dying. I couldn't make sense of it. Did I have to change my view of the man I loved? I wasn't sure I could, but how did this new information fit?

"I'm sorry I didn't tell you before this," Chris said. "But now you understand why I want to know if Vanessa is Terry's daughter. She has a right to know. Emmy has a right to know. Vanessa can decide on her own, when she gets older, if she wants to get tested for the disease. But she should know."

This statement brought a whole new world of awful possibilities crashing down. "Have you been tested?"

He shook his head. "No." When I didn't say anything, he continued. "I haven't wanted to know. It might make me live differently. More cautiously. Or more wildly. Make different decisions. I figure your time is your time. Nobody else knows when it's coming. I didn't want to know, either. I wanted more than anything else, for everything to be fine. Or at least to pretend it was."

I fought tears, blinking hard. Chris was the healthiest person I knew. His physical hard work outdoors kept him lean and well-muscled. His height and fitness had always made me feel safe in his presence, sheltered from whatever life threw at us. Now that feeling of safety was shattered. I was afraid. Afraid for him. Afraid for Vanessa. Afraid for us and the future.

Finally, the tears spilled over, splashing onto my plate. "I don't understand. Why are you just telling me now?"

"I couldn't talk about it before and I can't really talk about it now. I'm sorry." He stood, threw a twenty on the table, and stalked toward the door.

I left my pancakes uneaten and ran up the stairs to the studio. I hid my red nose behind a napkin as I left the restaurant. I didn't want friends or neighbors to see my splotchy, tear-stained face. My emotions were a jumble. I was mad and sad and hurt and scared, all at once.

I sat on our couch with my laptop and read about Huntington's Disease. None of it was good. The disease had no cure, and only minor treatments for symptoms. It was progressive and debilitating to both the mind and the body, including the loss of control of movement, ability to swallow, personality changes, loss of judgment and decision-making capabilities, spiraling into dementia. It was an equal oppressor of men and women. If either parent had the disease, the chances of a child inheriting it were fifty percent.

Symptoms appeared in the late thirties or early forties, unless they arrived much earlier. Chris was thirty-six. The earliest signs were subtle ticks in arms or legs, general clumsiness and jerky movements of the eyes. I thought hard about Chris, picturing conversations, interactions. One of the things that attracted me to him physically was his litheness, how he moved around his sailboat the *Dark Lady* with the grace of a well-muscled cat. No, I'd seen no sign of the disease yet.

The disease might move swiftly or slowly, but the end was the same, the requirement for full-time care. The average life expectancy after onset of symptoms was twenty years. I did the calculations in my head. Terry was ten years older than Chris, their sister in San Diego an unspecified number of years younger. Chris never spoke about her. Their mother had to be in her sixties, at least.

Of all the emotions and reactions stirring inside me, this simple set of facts caused the strongest reaction. Why did Chris never visit his mother? Their time was limited. And if she was too far into dementia to appreciate his presence, why did he never go to support his dad, whose life must be a hellish challenge?

Chris was a good man. A supportive man. Up until that moment, I'd believed that the biggest mistake he'd made in his life, smuggling prescription drugs from Canada for seniors in need, had been made out of kindness and generosity, not out of selfishness or greed.

But was there any other way to interpret Chris's actions? He never visited his parents, never called that I'd ever seen. For ten years, he'd never visited his brother in prison, though he was only an hour up the road. He never, ever mentioned his sister.

What could have happened? What had blown them apart?

My family had its conflicts, for sure. Sonny and I were opposite in every way—temperament, outlook, politics, religion—all the third rails of family conversation. Learning to run the Snowden Family Clambake together had been an adventure in daily confrontation. Livvie and I had spent most of our lives as opposites, too. I was the good girl, the student, the one who did everything her parents wanted. Livvie was the rebel, the flunker-outer, the girl who got pregnant her senior year in high school.

My parents had loved each other fiercely. We were always brought up to believe that the courtship and marriage of the girl on the private island and the boy who delivered groceries in his skiff was the stuff of fairy tales. It was the kind of love that forced everyone else out, including, occasionally, Livvie and me. My mother had mourned long and hard for my father, making little room in her sorrow for anyone but my niece Page.

We were a complicated family. Like every other family.

But when Livvie got pregnant, when my dad got cancer and died, and last year, when we'd almost lost the clambake business and Morrow Island to bankruptcy, we'd rallied. We'd fought and we'd yelled, but we'd rallied. And we also laughed and cried and hugged and said, "I love you." A lot. Because that's what families do.

Chris loved my family. There was a time when I'd worried he loved them more than he loved me.

He'd cheerfully, at his initiation, spent Thanksgiving
and Christmas, Easter and Fourth of July with us. He
loved being in the mix. He loved having a stocking
with his name on it hanging from my mother's
mantel with the rest of ours.

So why would he leave his father alone to deal
with his mother's illness? Why would he deprive
his mother of his presence and the comfort it
might bring? Wondering didn't lead me anywhere.
I'd have to ask him. When he calmed down.

I didn't know where he'd gone. To the *Dark
Lady*, probably. I was angry he'd run out on our
conversation, though there was no question in my
mind he'd left because of the topic, not because of
me. But until he could face his feelings, how was I
to know what they were? How could we truly be together?

The rain had slowed, but was still coming down,
the sky and the water were different shades of grey.
The giddy fun of a mid-season "snow day," had disappeared. The weather reflected my sadness and
confusion.

The information on the laptop told me ninety-
five percent of those who might have inherited the
disease chose not to be tested. There was no cure,
no effective treatment. The end was the same.
Testing lowered stress for both winners and losers,
but it also upped the chances of suicide.

The article helped me understand Chris's choice.
But if he didn't want to be tested, why then was he
determined that Emmy should know, and eventually Vanessa? Why should she be faced with the
same terrible knowledge, the same terrible choice?

I powered off the laptop and closed the lid. I was slightly more knowledgeable, but no wiser. I would have to wait for Chris for that.

I sat on the old couch for a few minutes more. I had no reason to move. No one needed me, no one wanted anything. So different from when I was at work. When I couldn't sit any longer, I pulled my slicker off the peg by the staircase and headed outside.

CHAPTER 16

It was too windy for an umbrella, so I hadn't grabbed one. The rain had slowed, but was still steady. I pulled the hood of my slicker up, put my head down, and made tracks for the town-hall-firehouse-police-station.

On the way up the walk to the police entrance, I ran straight into Duffy MacGillivray.

"Ooof! Julia, watch where you're going."

I backed up. "I'm so sorry Duffy, I was dodging the rain drops."

Duffy was a lobsterman and a bit of a Busman's Harbor character. Fortunately, in late middle age, the muscles he'd built up from hauling traps were well padded around his middle. He wasn't hurt and neither was I.

He squinted at me, appraising. "Where are you going in such a hurry?"

"Same place you just left, by the look of things."

He acknowledged I was right by the tip of his

head toward the double glass doors. "What's your business with them?"

It was an intrusive question; though I wasn't surprised he asked it. Duffy considered tact a waste of time.

"I need to speak to the detectives about Bartholomew Frick's murder." I figured my minor role in the murder was probably so well known around town that not answering his question would result in more rumors than answering it.

"Same," he grunted. "Good luck." I watched him lumber away. What could Duffy MacGillivray have to do with Bart Frick?

Inside, the door to the multi-purpose room was open about a foot. The receptionist inclined her head to indicate I should go in.

Binder and Flynn were alone, standing by a white board and talking in low tones. The moment he spotted me, Flynn flipped the board over, but not before I noticed a photo of Will Orsolini very near the center of the board, and one of Ida Fischer not far from it.

"What was Duffy MacGillivray doing here?" I asked.

Binder smiled. "Hello to you, too."

I reached their folding table desk at the same time they did, but neither sat. Binder held his hand out, gesturing toward the guest chairs in front of it. "Sit. Did you come to ask questions or do you have information that might actually be useful to us?" They were both smiling. We were one happy group. I wanted to keep it that way.

"I have information and questions," I assured them.

Binder removed his sports jacket and draped it across the back of his chair before he sat down. The storm outside had upped the humidity in the room. "In answer to your question, Mr. MacGillivray came in to provide Will Orsolini with an alibi. He says he saw Mr. Orsolini on the other side of Herrickson's Point at the relevant time."

That raised an interesting question. "What is the relevant time?"

"Between 11:05 AM and 11:34 AM," Flynn answered.

"That's precise."

"You gave us the 11:05 time," Binder reminded me.

"I was keeping track carefully that morning. I didn't want to miss the *Jacquie II*. How did you get the later time?"

"The call saying there was a body at Herrickson House came into 911 at 11:17 AM. Your friend Officer Dawes was first on the scene at 11:34 AM. Frick was dead when Officer Dawes found him."

"Who called 911?"

"Anonymous. From an extension inside the house."

Inside the house? That was creepy. "A man or a woman?" I asked.

"Man."

The hair on my arms stood up. "Do you think he was the killer? Because if he was, and he murdered Frick and called 911 twelve minutes after I left, that probably means—" I shuddered.

"He was already in the house when you were there," Flynn finished. "Yes, we believe the killer was."

I let that sink in. In the house with a killer. Herrickson House was enormous. So many places to hide. "What about Vera French? I told you she went onto the property as I left."

"She told us she went to the front door, knocked a few times, rang the bell, didn't get an answer and gave up. She claimed she was on and off the property in less than ten minutes." Binder sounded skeptical about Vera French's story, but then detectives were professional skeptics.

"So she was knocking on the door while the murder was going on? Where in the house was the body?"

"The body was in the breakfast room, one of the few places on the main floor not visible from the front porch," Flynn answered.

"Why call 911? The caller has helped you pinpoint the time of the murder. If he hadn't called, Frick might not have been found for days."

Ida Fischer had quit. The locked upper gates and chain link fence across the beach access road should have discouraged visitors. Should have, except if the cops were right, at least three of us, me, Vera French, and the killer, had come calling that morning.

"Very good question," Binder said. "We don't know why he called. The department psychologist says it might suggest the killer cared for Mr. Frick and wanted his body to be found before too much time went by."

"Cared for Mr. Frick? That doesn't describe anyone in Busman's Harbor."

"Or anyone else we've been able to find," Flynn added. "Not a popular guy."

Binder wriggled in his chair. He was a patient man, not given to fidgeting. I could tell my time to ask questions was up. "You said you had something for us?" he prompted.

"Yes. I don't know if it matters, but it's been bugging me. When I got to Herrickson House on the morning of the murder, I met Ida Fischer at the door, like I told you. She left it open and I went inside looking for Frick. I found him in Lou's study, examining an old letter from a pile of them on her roll top desk. When he saw me, he put the letter back in a hurry and slammed down the top of the desk. I had the feeling he didn't want me to see what he was reading."

When I finished speaking, they were silent. I had to admit, my information was underwhelming. "I thought you could at least maybe look at the letters," I finished. *Lame.*

Binder put on his glasses and typed into his laptop. I wondered if he'd taken me seriously or if it was a charade for my benefit. "Thank you, Julia. If there's nothing else—"

"Excuse me, Lieutenant." The civilian receptionist stood in the doorway. "There's some sort of trouble out at Herrickson Point. Officers Dawes and Howland are on the scene. The chief's on his way. He thinks you two should go as well."

Both men started for the door. "Do you have any more information?" Binder asked her.

"There's a crowd at the gate, threatening to pull it down," the receptionist told them. "It's getting heated."

In seconds, I was the only one left in the empty room. Sirens wailed from the parking lot. I pulled my slicker around me and ran for my car.

I reached Mom's garage and jumped into the Caprice. It was almost as wide as the doorframe, and I always had to ease her out slowly. Main Street was full of tourists practicing retail therapy as a way to soothe the rainy-vacation-day blues. I cursed as they meandered across the street, crossing without looking. As I edged my way through town, I also cursed the cops with their sirens and ability to make other vehicles get out of their way. They were probably already at Herrickson Point.

As I drove down Rosehill Road, I saw more than fifty people gathered at the turn onto the access road, even more than the day the gate had gone up. Cars and pickups littered both sides of the road. In the middle of it all, parked ten feet away from the gate, was the Barnard's RV with the distinctive silhouette of the lighthouse on the side.

The rain had slowed, but the wind was still high. It wasn't a good day for the beach.

I fought my way to the front of the crowd where Will stood nose-to-nose with Jamie, yelling at the top of his lungs. "Let us in. We've a right! Fishing, fowling, and navigation. This guy had no right to block us."

Jamie kept his voice even, trying to ratchet

down the tension. "We don't know if he had the right or not. That's why it's gone to court."

"And now he's dead," someone else shouted. "How long will we have to wait?"

Will spoke directly to Jamie who cupped his ear to hear in the wind. "You know this isn't what Lou wanted."

Jamie shook his head. "It's not Lou's decision anymore."

A grumble spread through the crowd. I looked around. The clammers held their rakes high. There were some beach goers, too, who lofted closed umbrellas. Vera French was in the crowd. It was too chilly for bathing suits. She was in white capris and a bright blue windbreaker. The gusts whipped her long, white hair around her face.

When she turned her head toward Herrickson House I did the same. Six big dark wood rockers lined the front porch, moving in the wind, as if occupied by ghosts.

Vera French's head swung back. She caught me staring and raised a hand in a half-hearted salute. Behind her, Glen Barnard stood on the top step of his RV, head and shoulders above the crowd.

All seven of Busman's Harbor's uniformed patrol officers were there, even Officer Larry, a retired cop From Away the BHPD hired every tourist season to help keep up with the paperwork. I'd never seen him outside of the station house. The buttons of his uniform shirt strained across his belly.

A siren blared on Rosehill Road. People moved aside and the chief's car pulled up next to the

Barnard's RV. Chief Beaupre hefted himself out of the driver's seat, looking, as always, annoyed. Beaupre's mood hit bottom on Memorial Day and he wouldn't smile again until Columbus Day. He had to deal with schedules, budgets, and the town selectmen, but other than that, his force was so small, he still had to go out on patrol. I wondered what part of our far-flung peninsula he'd been patrolling when he got the call about the mob at Sea Glass Beach.

Beaupre huddled with Jamie and the other officers. Then he motioned for Lieutenant Binder and Sergeant Flynn to join them. The crowd began to chant. "Let us in! Let us in! Let us in!" There was the *brrr* of a big engine revving. Glen Barnard was back behind the wheel of his RV, ready to roll, Anne at his side in the passenger seat.

"Let us in! Let us in! Let us in!" The clammers moved their rakes up and down with the rhythm of the chant.

Chief Beaupre nodded, and Jamie broke from the circle, fast walking through the crowd, back toward his patrol car parked on the road.

The chanting grew louder. Chief Beaupre faced the crowd and held up one hand, indicating he wanted to speak, but it was too late. The momentum of the crowd carried them forward, and people surged against the gate, beating it with the clam rakes. "Let us in! Let us in! Let us in!" Someone was going to get hurt. I wasn't the only one worried. A look passed between Chief Beaupre and Lieutenant Binder.

Jamie sprinted back with a big pair of bolt cut-

ters. "Let him through! Let him through!" someone at the back called out, and the crowd took up
the chant. Jamie moved slowly forward and posi-
tioned himself beside the middle padlock of three
on the gate. The crowd fell silent as he lifted the
big cutters and snapped the lock. A cheer went up.
"Hurray!" Jamie made quick work of the other two
locks.

The crowd surged forward, pushing the gate
out of the way. People poured into the parking lot,
shouting and cheering. The Barnards' RV came
through and drove to the other end of the lot by
the lighthouse.

Chief Beaupre stood on the boulder at the edge
of the parking lot and yelled over the wind. "Listen
up. This is temporary. Once we locate the heirs,
they may choose to close the gate again. If that happens, it goes back to court. In the meantime, I expect you to treat this property as if it were your
own, especially while that house is empty. Ya got
me?"

The group quieted. A few people nodded or
called out, "Yes."

"Good. It's a rotten day. Not good for swimming
or sunbathing. And it's high tide, so no clamming.
Everybody go home. Unless something unexpected happens overnight, the gate will be open
when you get here in the morning. Will, that okay
with you?"

Will nodded, and a few of the other clammers
chimed in. "Fine." "Okay." "No problem."

The rain picked up, dousing us all, its timing
perfect. People ran for their vehicles parked on

Rosehill Road. Except for the Barnards, whose RV at the end of the parking lot didn't move.

"I'll talk to them." Jamie pointed at the RV.

"Thanks," Binder responded. "Make sure they understand the rules. Beach access only. Not the light. Not the keeper's cottage. Not the mansion."

"Will do," Jamie said. "They'll be disappointed."

Binder was sympathetic. "At least they can get up close to it, even if they can't get inside."

The Caprice was so far up Rosehill Road, I was soaked by the time I reached it. The slicker protected my head and torso, but water wicked up my jeans. My canvas sneakers made squishing noises as I ran.

I was parked right in front of Vera French's gate. I hadn't seen her in the parking lot once the crowd got inside. She must have headed back to her house when Jamie cut the locks. I opened the gate to her cottage and followed the path toward the house.

The view from the lawn that rolled down to the boulders bordering the ocean was every bit as spectacular as I expected it to be. The architecture was so similar, I wondered if the cottage had once been an outbuilding of Herrickson House—a gardener's cottage or the home of some other faithful family retainer.

A screened-in porch ran across half the front of the cottage. Across the other half was an open deck, which was where the front steps deposited me. A lounge chair with big black wheels and a bright orange striped cushion sat on the deck, next to a table where cigarette butts floated in an ashtray filled with water by the rain.

The screen door on the porch was locked. I knocked and called. "Mrs. French? Yoo-hoo! It's Julia Snowden."

She came through the open front door of the house right away. "Julia. Hello." She opened the screen door and beckoned me in. "Please, call me Vera."

I followed her into the cottage, slipping off the soaking tennis shoes before I entered. She'd taken off the windbreaker. Her white capris and the pale-yellow blouse she wore were expensive-looking, but the cottage was anything but. The rough floor felt gritty with sand and dirt under my bare feet. The furniture was spare, and shabby. Not shabby-chic but shabby-shabby. The settee sagged; the coffee table was covered in cigarette burns. Through the living room archway, in the kitchen, an old soap-stone sink sat under the window. At some point in the distant past, someone had replaced its hand pump with a spigot and a pair of painted metal knobs. A big, single-door refrigerator wheezed in an alcove, but that was all the updating that seemed to have been done. The paint in both rooms was flat gray and dingy. The whole place reeked of tobacco smoke.

A kettle sounded on the stove and blew off a plume of steam. "I was making tea to try to warm myself after being on the beach. Would you like some? And maybe a few cookies?"

Despite the surroundings, my stomach rumbled. I'd walked out on breakfast after Chris left and hadn't stopped since. "Sure. Thanks."

She brought the tea in two mugs and a plate of Vienna fingers to the chrome-legged, linoleum-topped kitchen table and we sat. She looked at me expectantly.

I took a sip of the tea, buying time. "Before the kerfuffle on the beach, I was at the police station," I finally said. "They told me you didn't get to see Bart Frick on the day he died."

"I knocked and knocked and rang the bell. He didn't come. Maybe if he had, I would have been there with him when he was attacked and could have helped somehow."

"Or, you could have been killed."

"Or that." She wrapped her thin arms around her. "He was probably already dead when I got there. I heard the sirens from the first cop car before I was even back through my gate. I went upstairs to the bedroom and watched them all day—the cops, then the ambulance, more cops, the medical examiner."

"Yet you didn't come forward to say you'd been on the grounds."

She put both hands on her mug, warming them. "No. I wasn't anxious to tell them I'd been trespassing. You told them I was there." She gave a little smile. "I don't mind. It was the right thing to do."

Binder had said a man had called 911 from a phone inside Herrickson House, but listening to Vera's foghorn of a voice, I wondered. "You definitely didn't get inside?"

"No." She didn't seem offended by me asking. "I was disappointed at the time."

I took a Vienna finger from the plate and ate it, thinking about my next question. The cookie went down quickly and only made me hungrier. "You told me you'd never been in the house. It seemed odd to me because Lou was such a famous hostess," I said. My parents had been to parties at Herrickson House many times. Lou had slowed down in her final years. There had been no big parties by the time I was old enough to go, but Vera had told me she'd been a neighbor for more than two decades.

She gave me a sad smile. "I guess we weren't that kind of neighbors." Her eyes moved upward, in the direction of Herrickson House. It wasn't visible through the cottage windows. The hedges on both sides of Rosehill Road and the trees that lined the mansion's driveway blocked the view. "I wonder what will happen to it?" she said.

"I hope it stays as it is. That's what Lou wanted. And I hope whoever inherits lets people access the beach, like she did." My voice was more strident than I expected, taking me by surprise. I hadn't realized I cared so much.

"I hope so, too," Vera said. "Whoever it is."

Her comment brought me back to my thoughts from the night before. Who benefited from Bart Frick's death? Who owned the land, the lighthouse, the art, and antiques? Who owned Herrickson House now?

CHAPTER 17

I called my friend and attorney Cuthie Cuthbert-son from the road. Cuthie was a roly-poly man, always dressed in a too-big suit, his thick ma-hogany hair gelled within an inch of its life. But, despite these handicaps, he was one of the most successful criminal defense attorneys in Maine, the best in our county. People underestimated him, until he opened his mouth and used his beautiful baritone to tell the jury a convincing story. Cuthie was born to tell stories.

What he wasn't, was an estate lawyer. He didn't have the patience for wills and trusts. But he knew his way around a courthouse and around Maine's legal system. Besides, I couldn't think of anyone else to ask.

"What if someone died, and before their prop-erty was even probated, the heir died?" I asked.

"Is this a real case or a hypothetical?" Cuthie al-ways wanted to know where he stood.

"Real case."

"Heloise Herrickson, I'm assuming." He whistled. "So someone with significant property."

"Yes. The house and especially the property are valuable. And you should see the inside. It's like a museum—art, papers, jewelry, stamps, coins. It's amazing."

"I'm intrigued. Remind me, Lou died when?"

"Three weeks ago. She was a hundred and one."

"And she left the property to Bartholomew Frick, her grandnephew. Where was he from?"

"Brookline, Massachusetts."

"And he was murdered, what, three days ago?" Cuthie paused. "The news on Frick is probably not great. Unless his will was filed at the Registry of Probate down in whatever Massachusetts county he lived in before he died, you probably can't get access, unless you can figure out who his attorney is, and whoever that is would have no reason to tell you anything. Unless you're an heir. Why do you want to know this?"

I laughed. "No nothing like that." Though if I owned Herrickson House I would keep access to the beach open forever. "I can't help but wonder who owns the property now."

"Because maybe whoever it is would have a motive for murder."

I admitted it. "Well, wouldn't they? The state cops seem much more interested in the people who were on the scene and who wanted access to the beach."

"Then we must work to prevent a tragic miscarriage of justice." Ever the defense attorney, Cuthie was on board. "Here's my suggestion. Getting access to Frick's will is going to be a pain. You have a much better shot at finding Lou's. Frick may have already filed it at the Registry in Wiscasset. The way he put up that gate so fast, he seemed like a man in a hurry. He may have been the sole heir to the property on Herrickson Point, but there could have been personal bequests to others and so on. It might give you a sense of what other family is out there."

"That's a good idea."

"They're open 'til four. Any business in this for me?"

I laughed. "Yesterday I told Will Orsolini to call you before his second interview with the police, but he wouldn't go for it."

"I meant someone who could actually pay me, but thank you. Besides, I understand Will has a witness who can place him elsewhere at the relevant time."

"How the heck—?"

"I'm leaving lunch at Gus's right now. Duffy MacGillivray was there telling everyone who would listen about his central role in our local homicide. Such a drama queen. Good luck with your research."

The brick courthouse in Wiscasset sat high on the town green. I'd been by it countless times, but had never been inside. The Registry of Probate was a quick left after I came through the metal detector. I walked down the short hallway into a room lit with large windows even on a gray and rainy day.

The woman who helped me, Mrs. Hart, was patient and efficient. I'd been worried when I first walked in because everyone else there—sitting at the wooden table or standing at the high, blond wood counters—seemed to know exactly what they were doing. I was the only neophyte bumbling around, asking dumb questions.

Mrs. Hart told me proudly that the Registry had wills dating back to 1760, and that those filed in the last twenty years were digitized and available online. Heirs and executors (called Responsible Persons in Maine, as Jamie had already informed me) had anywhere up to three years to file a will for probate, so she couldn't guarantee Lou Herrickson's was there.

But, with a minimum of fuss, she retrieved a paper of copy of the will from somewhere behind a painted wooden door. Bart Frick had filed it the afternoon of his first day in town.

I went to the table and sat down next to a woman who had paper documents and file folders full of wills and estate inventories piled in front of her.

"Genealogy?" she asked me.

"No." Not wanting to be abrupt or unfriendly, I racked my brain for a more expansive response. I didn't think, "looking for a murderer," was going to do it. I settled on, "a family matter," which I supposed it was, though not my family. The woman gave me a pleasant smile and turned back to her work.

The beginning part of Lou's will was straight-forward. She said she was Heloise Herrickson, the widow of Francis Herrickson, and was of sound mind and body. The will was dated ten years before her death and was drawn up by a well-known Portland, Maine, law firm.

Lou had left, as I already knew, the property, light-house, and dwelling known as Herrickson House, and all contents therein, to her husband's grand-nephew, Bartholomew Frick of Brookline, Massa-chusetts.

But then it got strange. She left all of this to Frick on the condition that he live at Herrickson House and leave the land, house, outbuildings, and the contents of the house substantially as they were at her death for the period of one year. Only then, after the year had passed, did he inherit the property outright. If Frick failed to meet these conditions, the property passed to "my late hus-band's goddaughter, Elizabeth Anderson of Scar-borough, Maine."

That stopped me cold. Who was Elizabeth An-derson and why was she potentially inheriting an enormous house and acres of oceanfront prop-erty? Lou hadn't expanded on that.

I remembered Frick had said, "I may have to live here . . ." on the morning of the murder. At the time it hadn't struck me as strange. But now I knew he literally had to live at Herrickson House if he hoped to get his inheritance. Did the gate he'd put across the beach road constitute an alteration? From a structural point of view it was easily taken down, clearly temporary. But its spirit altered the property substantially, blocking access Lou and generations of Herricksons had allowed.

Frick was the Responsible Person as well as the heir, which seemed a bit like putting the fox in charge of the henhouse. He would be the one to attest that he had lived in Herrickson House for a year and that he had not substantially altered the property or the house, or sold the contents for that matter. Except he wouldn't, because he was dead.

There were a few other bequests. Five thousand dollars each to Lou's hairdresser, handyman, cleaning lady, and gardener. Not a life-changing amount, but an amount that would no doubt come in handy in the long winter months ahead. Twenty-thousand to the Art League in the hopes they would make improvements and repairs to their gallery building. An endowment to the high school to give a scholarship to a promising art student in her name.

Lou left a hundred thousand dollars to Ida Fischer, along with the wish that Ida be "allowed to live at Herrickson House for as long as she wishes. It has become her home." Ida had lasted exactly one day after Bart Frick arrived. The amount was generous, certainly, but it wouldn't last forever, especially without the free housing that Lou had wished for her, and it was hard to imagine Ida could get another job at her age. She'd been a companion to Lou more than anything, making simple meals and doing light housekeeping. Others came in to do the heavy lifting.

And then, in one of the final paragraphs of the will, something else shocked me. "I have deliberately and consciously left nothing to my daughter, for reasons well known by her."

Daughter? No one had ever mentioned a daughter. And, what could a daughter have done that everything was left to a grandnephew of Lou's late husband? I could see maybe the real estate should go to a "Herrickson," but what about the art and other treasures? They must be worth a fortune. Lou was so famously generous. What on earth would have made her turn her back on her own child?

And who was this mysterious Elizabeth Anderson of Scarborough, Maine? If she inherited an estate worth millions on Frick's death, wasn't she suspect number one? But did she inherit? Frick hadn't lived out his year at Herrickson House, that was certain. But he'd been unable to, because he was murdered. So did the estate pass to Elizabeth Anderson or did it pass to Bart Frick's heirs, whoever they might be?

The rest of the will was routine. I didn't recognize the names of either witness. It had probably been signed in the lawyer's office.

I made some notes on my phone and gave the document back to the nice clerk, pulled my slicker over my head and dodged the rain as I raced to my car. Inside, it was like a sauna. The windows were fogged and the rain decreased visibility to zero.

I'd gone looking for other suspects in Bart Frick's murder and I'd found two. Elizabeth Anderson, who inherited, if she inherited. Her motive was clear. And the mysterious daughter. If Bart Frick was dead, she still didn't get anything, but wouldn't that make you crazy if you were Lou's daughter?

I had the feeling Lou didn't know Bart Frick well if she thought he was the type of person who would happily let Ida Fischer live in his house for free. Or, if she thought he would keep the house as it was, instead of selling of her treasures, tearing Herrickson House down, and building oceanfront McMansions. (Filet-O-Fish Houses?) If you were Lou's daughter, and you knew that all the money in the estate, everything except the real estate, came from your mother, and yet your mother had plucked an obscure relative of her husband's and given him everything, what would you do?

I turned the key in the ignition and put the defroster on full blast, for all the good it did. I gave up, opened the windows in spite of the rain, and when the windshield cleared, headed back to Busman's Harbor.

CHAPTER 18

On the way back, I called Sergeant Tom Flynn on his cell.

"Julia. Chatting with you twice in one day. This is becoming a habit."

"I was over at the courthouse looking at Heloise Herrickson's will," I told him. No point in holding back.

"Were you now?" Flynn seemed more amused than upset.

"I was. I assume you know what the will says."

"Of course." Flynn still played along.

"So it seems to me Elizabeth Anderson is an obvious suspect in Bart Frick's murder."

"Obvious," Flynn confirmed.

When he didn't expand, I asked, "Is that something you're pursuing?"

"We would be. If we knew where she was."

"You don't know where she is?"

"Nope." Flynn blew out a puff of air. "No Elizabeth Anderson in Scarborough, according to the town clerk. We checked with the local police department. They've never heard of her. They were nice enough to knock on the doors of all the Anderson families in town. Nothing."

"The lawyer who drew up Lou's will must know who Elizabeth Anderson is."

"He doesn't. Ten years ago Mrs. Herrickson gave him the name and phone number of a private detective she said would be able to put the attorney in touch with Ms. Anderson should the need ever arise. The PI has given up his license and left the state. We've heard he's somewhere in Florida. We're trying to get in touch. In the meantime, we've tried DMV records, arrest records. I've taken to random Googling."

I imagined high-energy Flynn stuck at his desk clicking on the results from a search engine. It must be driving him crazy. "So does Elizabeth Anderson inherit or do Frick's heirs?"

"Do I sound like an estate attorney? Mr. Frick appears to have died intestate, in any case."

"Without a will?"

"It's not that uncommon. Frick was in his forties, healthy, no wife or kids. And, until three weeks ago, he didn't have much. A modest condo, a four-year-old car."

"He was driving a hundred thousand dollar Porsche."

"Bought two weeks ago at a shady dealership using his coming inheritance as collateral. Frick probably would have made a will now that he was a multimillionaire, but he hadn't gotten around to it yet."

"So that means?"

"I'm not a judge, but I'm guessing this Elizabeth Anderson inherits because Frick didn't spend his year at Herrickson House."

"Doesn't that make her your chief suspect?"

"Not if she never turns up to collect."

I had to give that one to Flynn. Killing to inherit wasn't a motive if you never put your hand up to say, "It's mine."

"And the daughter, the one who was disinherited?" I asked.

"We have the Palm Beach PD looking," Binder answered. "We're assuming she's Mrs. Herrickson's child with her first husband, Charles Mills, but we're still verifying. The daughter may well have a married name."

"Or an alias," I said. "I'm not sure I'd keep my parent's name if she treated me like that. Lou was a hundred and one when she died, so the daughter would be . . ."

"Yeah," Flynn confirmed. "Seventies or eighties. Or perhaps deceased herself."

"Why go to the trouble of disinheriting someone who's already dead?"

"The will's ten years old," he reminded me. "The daughter could have died anytime since it was made. You never heard anything about a daughter?"

"Nothing. If anyone knows, it's Ida Fischer."

"Ms. Fischer is coming in later today. We have many reasons for wanting to talk to her."

I remembered Ida's photo on the whiteboard when Flynn had turned it over.

"Could a woman have committed this murder?"

I asked. "An older woman?" Ida Fischer was an older woman. Lou's disinherited daughter was an older woman. Frank Herrickson was born in 1909, so the missing Elizabeth Anderson, his goddaughter, was probably an older woman, too. Certainly she was a woman. If she was alive.

"The room where Frick was killed was a wreck," Flynn told me. "There was broken china and glass, shattered pictures. Like whoever it was came in there swinging the weapon in fury, taking out everything in their path. We think whoever it was took an overhead swing and happened to hit him exactly right. A lucky shot."

"Not so lucky for him."

"He had no defensive wounds. We're not sure why he didn't put his hands up, try to deflect the blow. But in answer to your question, yes a woman could have done it."

"Thanks," I said.

"Happy to be of service, ma'am."

I knocked on the door of Ida Fischer's sister's house. It was a modest two-story on a tiny lot in the center of Busman's Harbor. I didn't know her sister, but in the way of small towns, I knew of her. The sister had a husband, a middle-aged daughter, and son still living at home, three daughters living nearby, and a passel of grandchildren. I imagined Ida's presence made the house feel pretty crowded.

It was Ida who answered the door. "Julia."

"Hi Ida. I wanted to follow up on our conversation at the Snuggles. Do you mind if I come in?"

"Of course, of course. Peg and I were just sitting down for a cold drink on a muggy day. I can't talk long. I'm expected at the police station. Come in." She led me through a small living room crowded with giant brown furniture into a kitchen just large enough to hold an eating table.

"Do you know my sister Peg?" she asked.

"Don't get up. I'm Julia." Ida's sister Peg was her physical opposite in every way. Where Ida was small and tough, like a buzzard, Peg was big and soft, like a farm-raised turkey.

"I know you. You're Jacqueline's daughter."

"Yes, that's right. Pleased to meet you."

"Fee and Vee asked Julia to help out with my little problem," Ida told her.

"You mean your problem of being suspected of murder . . . again." Peg sure didn't pull any punches.

"I wouldn't say suspected," Ida protested. Would she have been so sure if she'd known her photo was on the whiteboard down at the police station?

"Humph." Peg was not impressed.

Peg stood and pulled a glass from a cabinet. She filled it with ice and poured cold tea over it. She bustled about, cutting a wedge of lemon, getting a spoon. "There's sugar and the pink packets on the table," she said, pointing with her knuckle. She sat back down.

"That's what I've come to see you about. Do you know about the provisions of Lou's will?" I asked Ida.

"Her attorney called me to tell me about the hundred thousand dollars, if that's what you mean."

"And the part where she said she hoped Bart Frick would let you live out your life in Herrickson House?"

She nodded. "Yes. But the attorney said it was only that, a wish, unenforceable if Mr. Frick chose to ignore it. Besides, I left. He didn't throw me out. I couldn't have spent the rest of my life with that odious man."

"Which is what makes you suspect numero uno," Peg pointed out. "Well, this, that, and the other thing."

Peg stood up and went to the refrigerator. She pulled out a bowl with plastic wrap over its top. "I'm stress eating for two," she said as she removed the plastic. "Ida here is stress non-eating." She inclined her head toward her wiry sister.

She put the bowl, full of something thick and white, on the table along with an open bag of corn chips. Sitting down again, she scooped a chip into the dip and popped it into her mouth. "My famous clam dip," she said when she finished chewing. "Have some."

The Vienna finger I'd had with Vera French wasn't cutting it. I followed Peg's lead. The dip was wonderful, somehow both creamy and chewy, and bursting with the flavor of the sea. I was so hungry, I could have eaten the whole bowl. As Peg had predicted, Ida didn't touch a single chip. I needed to get the conversation back on track. I helped myself to one more delicious dip and soldiered on.

"Did Lou's lawyer tell you about the other provisions of the will? Or perhaps you already knew them because you and Lou were so close."

"I didn't know about the will. Lou was outgoing but you shouldn't confuse that with being open. There were parts of our lives where Lou kept her secrets, and I kept mine. She told me I'd be taken care of and I believed her."

"Bah!" The word burst from Peg's pursed lips. "One hundred thousand, for thirty years of service. If she paid you better and you'd had an IRA, you would have been better off than that. As it is, you don't even have enough money to re-house yourself."

"She didn't think I'd have to re-house myself, did she?" Ida still defended her late employer. "She thought I'd be living at Herrickson House. With the money Lou left and my social security, I can rent a place in the off season," Ida swallowed, "and maybe stay here in the summer?"

"Bah," Peg repeated. "You know you're always welcome here. But you shouldn't have to depend on family."

"Who knows how long I'll live?" Ida responded. "Maybe I should blow it all in one crazy year."

Peg shook her head. "Don't even joke."

"Did you know Bart Frick?" I asked. "Was he a frequent visitor at Herrickson House when Lou was alive?"

"I never laid eyes on him until he showed up on your boat," Ida answered. "Right after that, he moved into the mansion. It was all downhill from there. I met his grandparents, back when I worked for the Herricksons the first time. She was Frank Herrickson's sister." Ida closed her eyes. "I'm trying to remember if I ever met his parents. I don't think so."

"So why did Lou leave the property to someone she'd never met?"

Ida sighed. "She was following Frank's wishes. Frank left everything to her when he died, but his will said that if she predeceased him, everything was to go to this grandnephew, Bartholomew Frick."

"Lou was so attached to Busman's Harbor. I thought perhaps she'd leave the land to the town," I said.

"The *Herricksons* were quite definite that a *Herrickson* should always be at *Herrickson* Point," Ida replied, emphasizing the Herrickson each time she spoke it. "Old Mrs. Herrickson, Frank's mother, was a dragon on that point. As she was a dragon in so many other ways."

"She was a tartar, that one," Peggy confirmed. "The stories Ida used to bring to Sunday supper, back in the day."

Ida smiled a thin smile.

"And then there's Lou's daughter." I brought the conversation back to the will. "Why would she cut out her own flesh and blood?"

Ida shifted in her seat. "I don't know. I told you, Lou and I kept our secrets." She stopped, looking up at me. I didn't say a word, hoping she would go on. She did. "It had something to do with Frank. The daughter, who was an adult at the time, objected to their marriage. Lou married him anyway and never forgave her."

Across the table, Peg said. "Imagine. Turning your back on your own child. No matter what her age."

"That seems like a draconian response to a common objection to a second marriage," I said.

"It was Lou's fifth, actually," Ida corrected. "For the record. But it lasted almost thirty years and would have lasted longer if Frank hadn't died."

"Did either of the Herricksons ever mention the name Elizabeth Anderson?" I asked.

Ida frowned, thinking hard. "No, never that I can recall."

"An Elizabeth Anderson never came to the house?"

"That I'm sure of. Never. At least never while I was present."

I stood to go. "Thanks, Ida. This has been very helpful. Good luck with the police. If you think you should have an attorney present, my friend Cuthie Cuthbert is excellent."

"I've been telling her to get an attorney," Peg said.

"Pshaw. I'll be fine."

"Nice to meet you, Peg," I said. "Thanks so much for the iced tea and the delicious dip."

Ida walked me to the door. "I don't see how that could have been helpful."

"It was," I assured her.

Gus's was closed, all the lights off, and the hushed, dark interior of the restaurant made me feel dreary on a dreary day. Chris wasn't home. There were no messages on my phone. Upstairs in the apartment there was nothing on the old, white refrigerator where we left notes for one another. I imagined he was on the *Dark Lady*, alone with his thoughts, as I was alone with mine.

I sent him the simple text, HOME and stared at my phone's screen, hoping for a response. Crickets.

I fixed myself some peanut butter crackers. The cupboard was bare. In the summer, we ate no meals at home. I knew Gus wouldn't mind if I helped myself to a hotdog or a hamburger from his walk-in. He'd encouraged me to do that many times, but, hungry as I was, it seemed like more trouble than it was worth.

To distract myself from things I couldn't change, I searched for Elizabeth Anderson. Flynn had said he'd searched the web, but I was more confident in my skills than I was in his. During my years away from Busman's Harbor when I'd worked in venture capital in Manhattan, I'd researched the companies my firm had invested in, their management and angel investors. There was a saying in my office that if Julia couldn't find it, it wasn't on the web.

Lou's will had said Elizabeth Anderson was Frank Herrickson's goddaughter. That probably meant that at least one of her parents had been a friend of his, probably the dad. Town friend? Prep school friend? College friend? Frank had been older than Lou. A child born to a school friend of his might well be in her eighties or even nineties. Would Lou have left Herrickson House and everything in it to someone of that advanced age, even as a contingency? I didn't think so. Lou was a practical person.

I didn't know much about Frank. He'd died when I was a girl. I'd always pictured him living out his long bachelor years at Herrickson House waiting for Lou to come along so he could fall in love with her. But during that time, he'd been a lawyer in Portland, Ida had said the first time we'd talked.

I started off with a garden-variety search for background. *Ah ha!* Francis Herrickson had specialized in real estate law. Citations to his cases, which had been digitized, showed he'd handled boundary disputes, title problems, competing claims of ownership that had gone to litigation. It was ironic given an injunction had just been filed in such a case regarding his own land.

His firm's name had been Herrickson and Carroll, and I spent a fruitless half an hour trying to see if his partner Carroll, who I assumed was deceased, had any children. Who more obvious to name as the godfather to your child than your law partner? Carroll had died in 1954, and his obituary mentioned no wife or children. Evidently, during the years of their partnership, both men had been confirmed bachelors. I pictured them like Scrooge and Marley in their counting house.

That left me at a dead end. I got up and paced around. Ida Fischer had said she'd never heard of Elizabeth Anderson. She'd known Frank even before Lou did. Of course there would be a big gap in her knowledge while she'd been in prison. Maybe even longer, since she'd left old Mrs. Herrickson's employ and Busman's Harbor when she got married.

The gloomy day had gotten gloomier. I put on the light next to the couch and sat down again. I needed another approach. I tried searching for the name "Francis Herrickson," combined with "baptism," "christening," "godfather" and "godchild" and got nowhere.

I was ready to give up, but then I thought, if Lou wanted to leave virtually her entire estate to someone, it had to be someone important to Frank. There would be some memento of the relationship certainly. I closed my eyes and thought about my tour of Herrickson House. Had there been a photo of Frank with a child or holding a baby?

I'd been on such sensory overload when I was there. There had been generations of photos on every side table, and lining some of the bookshelves, but I didn't remember any photos of children, none at all. Which was odd, because in my experience people took more photos of children than they did of adults. My brother-in-law Sonny had a saying, "In this family, if you want your picture taken, stand next to a kid." And it was doubly odd because Lou had a kid. She'd cut her daughter out of her life, but not to retain any reminders of her childhood?

I fell asleep like that. In the corner of the couch, my computer on my lap. At some point, I woke up long enough to turn it off and put it on the coffee table.

Chris never came home.

CHAPTER 19

I woke up to the gyrations of my cell phone on the coffee table. I uncurled myself from my fetal position on the couch and answered without looking at the display. I assumed it was Chris.

"Hi!" I did my best to sound chipper.

"Julia? You're up."

"Quentin? What time is it?"

"Almost eight. I'm glad I got a hold of you. I heard the gate across the beach road at Herrickson Point is open. Wyatt's dying to see Herrickson House."

My brain, just coming alive, was slow to compute. "You won't be able to get into the house. It's a crime scene."

"We can at least walk around and look in the windows. Meet us there in half an hour."

Half an hour? "I'm not even dressed." I was dressed, but in yesterday's clothes.

"Well, get dressed. See you there."

I double-timed my way through my morning rou-

tine. The sun shone through the studio windows.
A nice day meant going back to work. While I'd
enjoyed having the day off as much as the next person, the bills would pile up quickly if we weren't
open for business. And our employees relied on
tips. No work, no tips.

When I was dressed, I went downstairs, slipped
out the back door of Gus's and ran to my mother's
garage. I pulled the Caprice out and headed to
Herrickson Point.

That Chris hadn't come home worried and upset
me. Not so much the not sleeping at the apartment
part. He stayed on the *Dark Lady* from time to time
when chores kept him there late in the evening, or
when he'd been tied up at his job at Crowley's and
then driving his cab. But he'd always texted me to
let me know where he was.

It was the way we'd parted that was the problem.
He didn't want to talk about his family or the disease they carried. It had taken everything he had
in him to tell me what he did. I could see it, and
felt awful for him. To a point. Because, fundamen-
tally, he wasn't being fair to me. He hadn't told me
about his mother. He hadn't told me he might get
sick, too. No matter what happened between us
from here on out, we loved each other now. He
should have told me sooner.

Chief Beaupre had been true to his word. The
gate to the beach parking lot stood open. Half a
dozen clammers worked down by the waterline. I
recognized Will by his stance and physique, but
didn't call to him. He wouldn't have heard me
over the surf. Quentin's antique wood-sided estate

wagon was already in the parking lot. He and Wyatt leaned against it, waiting for me.

After I parked, we walked up the driveway to Herrickson House. When we reached it, Wyatt bounded up the front steps, walked along the deep porch and tried the front door. It was locked, as I was sure it would be.

"I'm going to try the other doors." Wyatt went back down the steps and started around the side of the house.

"You can't go in!" I called after her. "Chief Beaupre specifically said no one in the house."

Wyatt didn't answer. Quentin hesitated for a moment and then followed. I was left alone on the big front porch.

There were more than a dozen other doors to examine—the French doors to the dining room, kitchen door, back hall door, sun porch door, and on the ground floors, doors fixed in the thick stonewalls to the old laundry, coal room, cold food storage pantry, and workshops. They'd be gone for a while.

I decided to use the time to look through the windows for a photo of Frank Herrickson with a baby. All the public rooms at the front of the mansion could be inspected from the front porch. I started at the living room. As I remembered, there were photos on every available surface. Long lives, well lived, or at least that's what I'd assumed when I'd first seen them. Some of the photos were on side tables and faced away from me. Others were perched on bookcases all the way across the room, too small for me to see. I cupped my hand over my eyes and pressed my face to the glass to get a better look.

A man's torso loomed in front of me. "Aiiyyeee!"

"Julia! Julia!" The torso disappeared and seconds later Quentin opened the front door and stepped onto the porch. "It's me. Wyatt found a door in the cellar that had been propped open with a rock. Come inside."

"You nearly gave me a heart attack! You realize the last time I was in this house there was probably a murderer hiding somewhere."

That wiped the smile off his face. We stood in the oval front hall. "Where's Wyatt?" I demanded.

"Somewhere deep in the house rapturously taking photos of woodwork, or door knobs, or something," he answered.

"We can't be in here. Wyatt!" I shouted. "Wyatt!" My voice echoed through the cavernous rooms.

"We have to find her," I said to Quentin. I was annoyed with both of them. The house was a crime scene for heaven's sake. And if the cops discovered we'd been in there, they might block beach access again, which would anger the entire town. "You go upstairs. I'll look down here. And for goodness sake, don't touch anything and tell Wyatt not to touch anything."

When Quentin left me, I went through the archway into the dining room. "Wyatt?" She wouldn't have gone into the breakfast room, would she? The murder room. I shuddered, hugging myself as I stepped forward to peer through the doorway, just in case.

I stared into the sun-filled room. It was a wreck,

as Flynn had described. Broken shards of china
and glass sat on the hutch and sideboard and the
floor around them. Art hung crazily askew on the
walls. The Oriental carpet was gone, probably
taken by the crime scene techs, but the shadow of
a pool of blood remained on the hardwood floor.
Someone had wiped it up, but the rest of the
cleanup remained for the new owner. If she was
ever found.

The rest of the house looked like nothing had
happened. The murderer's rage had been con-
fined to that single space.

I returned to the oval-shaped front hall. I could
hear footsteps above and the faint sound of Quentin's
voice calling Wyatt. I went through the archway and
crossed the living room, pausing on my way to
look carefully at the photos as I went. My impression from my previous visit that there were no
photos of children was confirmed.

In Lou's study, I went to her desk. Its roll top
was closed. I put my hand on the top, which jiggled beneath it. It wasn't locked. Taking a deep
breath, I rolled the top back.

The letters were gone!

I was disappointed, but also relieved. Binder
and Flynn must have thought my clue was important and picked the letters up after all.

As long as I was there, I poked around a bit in
the desk. It was a beautiful oak with all sorts of
nooks for correspondence, pens, cards, and other
doodads. There wasn't much to see. A skeleton key
in one cubby that probably fit the lock for the

desktop, some return address labels in a fancy font. Evidently, for all her collecting, Lou hadn't been much for keeping desk sorts of things. Except, of course, for those letters.

Then my eye caught a corner of grey metal sticking out on the writing surface of the desk, like something was pushed beneath the lowest row of cubbies. I put a cautious finger on it and fished it out. It was an old silver frame, very tarnished, with a rough, moss green velvet backing. My heart beat faster. I turned it over.

It was a photo of Frank Harrington with a little girl. I recognized him because of all the photos all around the place. The child in his arms was perhaps two years old, blonde and plump cheeked, smiling at the camera. Frank smiled too, beamed actually, as he lifted her on his shoulder. She wore a fancy dress with smocking across the chest. It seemed to me even in the black and white photo that the dress must be white. Behind her were bushes and a gate, and little parts of people caught by the camera, an elbow, a fancy hat. They were at a party of some sort.

Could it be a christening? The child seemed a little old, but everything else was right—a daytime celebration, a white dress, Frank holding the child for a photo.

I sank into the leather-padded desk chair. Perhaps there was something on the back of the photo. A name, a date, a clue as to some other aspect of the mysterious Elizabeth Anderson's identity. I had to tug hard to slide the moss green back off the silver frame, which had become misshapen over time. It took three tries, but at last the thing came free. I slid the photo out.

There was nothing on the back. Absolutely nothing.

I sighed, disappointed, and began reassembling the photo and frame, reversing the previous process. I'd been so sure I was onto something.

When the photo was back in the frame I turned it over, examining it one last time. It felt like the image was screaming at me, begging me to decipher it and I could not.

"There you are. Aren't you the one who told us about a hundred times not to touch anything? Yet, here you sit at Lou Herrickson's desk like Lady Muck." Quentin's scolding tone said one thing, but his grin said another. Probably because of my own guilty feelings, it took me a second to realize he was teasing. The heat rose in my cheeks.

"Sorry!" I moved the photo to one hand and slammed down the desktop with the other.

"Don't apologize to me. What have you got there?"

I cleared my throat, which was suddenly dry. "Nothing."

He didn't hide his disbelief. "Yeah, right. Anyway, I was looking for you to tell you I found Wyatt. She's on the front porch."

"Okay. Be right out!" Why was my voice so loud? So cheery? "You guys go ahead. I have my own car."

Quentin didn't seem to notice. He turned and headed for the door. I stood up from the chair and pushed it back under the desk. Then, at the very last moment, trying not to think too much, I put the photo in my tote bag.

I flopped into one of the rockers on the porch and waited until Wyatt and Quentin were nearly to the parking lot before I slid the framed photo out of my bag.

I studied it carefully. Frank and the toddler were at an outdoor party. I could get that from the scene behind them, the parts of people. Frank's expression was tender; his eyes framed by his thick black glasses were wistful. He was older when it was taken, somewhere deep in middle age. Was he regretting his bachelor status, wishing for a child?

The scene behind them, rendered in grayscale, looked eerily familiar. Where was it? I zoomed through my memories. Boxwood hedges and a particular gate. The gate to the house across Rosehill Road where Vera French lived.

I put my hand on the glass to block out the shadows and strained to see. It was the gate, definitely, and behind it, far in the background, was a piece of the second story of Herrickson House. The trees along the driveway didn't yet block the view. Frank and the little girl were on the inside of the gate, in Vera French's yard. Which meant, if it was indeed a christening celebration, and it was held across the street at Vera French's house, weren't the owners likely to be the child's parents? Or at least a close relative or friend.

I went around to the back of Herrickson House

and found the cellar door Wyatt and Quentin had entered through, which was propped open with a rock. I pushed the stone out of the way with my sneakered foot. The door swung shut. I wrapped the fabric of my tote bag around my hand and tried the knob. The door hadn't locked. I opened it again to see if I could lock it from the inside, but when I turned the latch, the door wouldn't close. I shut it again to see if I could get it to latch from the outside, but no dice. I was surprised the police hadn't secured it in some way.

There were so many valuables in the house, I worried about leaving it unlocked. I felt around the outside doorframe. It wouldn't have been an unusual thing in Busman's Harbor to lock a door but leave a key easily accessible for delivery and repair people who might enter through the basement. But my fingers scraped along the chipped paint, finding nothing.

Finally, I closed the door behind me. I moved the rock that had propped it open back to the small bald spot on the lawn by the stoop where it had obviously come from. As I did, I spotted the impression of a skeleton key in the earth. So, there had been a key. But whoever had been in the house before us had taken or moved it.

I wasn't going to call the police and tell them the house was unsecured. That would result in way too many questions. Feeling a little sick, I walked down the path to the pedestrian gate. Holding the photo in my hand, I studied the green gate to Vera's property across Rosehill Road. I was sure it was the one, though the photo had been taken from inside the yard looking out.

I walked through the pedestrian gate, closing it carefully behind me to make sure it locked. Then I crossed Rosehill Road and entered Vera's yard. Using the photo, I was able to figure out exactly where Frank had stood on the lawn with the child in his arms.

Could that little girl have been Vera French, living here all along? No, that didn't make sense. Vera wasn't a diminutive of Elizabeth. Vera had said she'd never been inside Herrickson House. And, Vera had said she and Lou had been neighbors for more than twenty years, but the clothes in the photo were much older than that—fifty years or more.

But maybe Vera had bought the house from Elizabeth Anderson or her parents? She was the best lead I had. I turned toward the cottage to find Vera.

CHAPTER 20

"Who's that?" Vera French's voice came from the wooden lounge chair with big wheels at the back and the orange striped cushion on the deck. I could barely see her from where I stood.

"Julia Snowden," I answered.

Vera didn't get up or even sit up. "Come here where I can see you."

I climbed the steps to the deck. She was prone on the lounge chair and wore a bathing suit covered with big, splotchy blue and purple flowers. A smart phone, a pack of cigarettes, and a pair of Bluetooth ear buds sat on the table beside her.

"What can I do for you?" She asked it in a welcoming tone, not at all challenging.

"I've come to ask about your house."

"My house?" Her face knotted in confusion. "This house? What about it?"

Well, that was the rub. "I'm interested in people who used to live here. How long have you owned it?"

"I don't own it, dearie. I rent. This is my twenty-second season."

"Who owns it?" I asked.

Her right eyebrow shot up. "You're not thinking of renting it, are you?" She clearly didn't want competition.

"No, no. At least not during the season."

"Not during the off season, either. It's not winterized. I leave every year at the end of September, and believe me, by then it's plenty cold."

"I hear you." I persisted. "Your cottage looks a lot like Herrickson House. I wonder if it might have been a part of the original estate. Do you know who the owners are?"

"I deal with a management company out on the highway, Oceanside Realty. The owner of the cottage may be named on the rental agreement. I don't honestly remember."

"Do you mind checking?"

"Oh goodness, dear," she waved an airy hand, "I wouldn't know where to begin to look."

Oceanside Realty was on the two-lane highway that led from Route 1 down the peninsula to Busman's Harbor. The agency had been there as long as I could remember and was pretty much the only place in town for home sales or seasonal rentals. The owners had once had a corner on weekly and monthly rentals, too, but those had moved mostly to online services like Airbnb.

There was one car in the small parking lot. I

pulled the Caprice next to it and went inside. A woman about my age got up from behind a desk and came to the counter. The nametag on her blouse said MOLLY. "Can I help you?"

"I'm here about a property. It's on Rosehill Road right across from the Herrickson estate."

"I know the one. Were you interested in renting? Because we have a long-term tenant there during the season."

I shook my head. "Actually, I want to know who the owner is."

Her eyelids half closed with suspicion. "Why? If you're thinking you can cut some sort of a deal with the owner to rent or buy, you should know, we have an exclusive arrangement."

"No, no, nothing like that. I'm looking into the history of the house. I'm trying to get in touch with the owner. It may even be a prior owner I need to speak to."

She relaxed a little. "I don't know anything about the history of the cottage. It's been on our books forever. Since long before I got here. We do the maintenance, you know, cut the grass, trim the hedge, close the place up in the fall, open it in the spring. The minimum really. There's no sense in doing any more. The tenant says she likes it as it is."

"Is there anyone else I can speak to—one of the owners of the agency perhaps?"

"I doubt they could help. If you want to know the history of the house, why don't you see Mark Hayman in the Code Enforcement Office? He knows every property in town."

"Of course, you're right. Mark Hayman. Why didn't I think of him?" I thanked her and headed for the door.

"Good luck," Molly called.

"Thanks. I think I'll need it."

Town was full of tourists, jaywalking, weaving in and out of stores, carrying heavy parcels. The Caprice's dashboard clock had stopped working sometime in the last millennium and I didn't dare risk glancing at my phone until I pulled into the parking lot at the town office building. When I stopped, I was glad to see I had time to run in and give Binder and Flynn the photo. I was feeling guilty carrying it around.

But the civilian receptionist said both men stayed in Augusta for the day, so I went across the hall to talk to Mark Hayman in the town's Code Enforcement Office.

Mark's was the office that gave approvals to people for construction projects. If it was something simple, an addition to a house on a lot that was large enough for it, he could give the approval himself on behalf of the town. If it was a use that didn't conform to existing zoning, the case would have to go before the planning board. Mark was the person who gave you that bad news and walked you through the process. He'd been the Code Enforcement Officer for more than thirty years, and he had an encyclopedic knowledge of every building in town.

"How can I help you, Julia?"

"I'm interested in a house on Rosehill Road."

His gray eyebrows traveled upward toward his gray hairline. "Thinking of buying? I thought Chris still had the cabin."

Chris did, as Mark well knew. He wouldn't have missed that transaction. Even in my second summer back in Busman's Harbor, I was still adjusting to the fact that a relative stranger, someone I didn't socialize with at all knew, a) who my boyfriend was and b) what property my boyfriend owned.

"No, no. I'm doing some research," I assured him.

He nodded. It was nothing to him. "Which house?"

"The house with the rosebushes over the green gate." I paused. "Across from Herrickson House."

"Ah, Spencer Cottage." Mark sat at his desk and typed something into his computer. "Hmm. As I thought. Owned by the Spencer Family Trust. There's a seasonal tenant there, if I recall correctly."

Of course he recalled correctly. "Vera French," I confirmed. "She rents from Oceanside Realty."

Mark shrugged. That was none of his concern.

"Is there anything more you can tell me about the Spencer Family Trust?" I asked.

Mark scanned the screen. "It's an oldie. The trust has owned the property since 1965."

The nineteen-sixties. That seemed like the right era for the photo of Frank Herrickson and the little girl. "Do you have the name of the trustees? Or maybe the previous owner? Or the beneficiary?"

He looked at the screen again. "Previous owner, I don't know. At some point the cottage was part of the Herrickson estate. Trust beneficiaries," he looked at the screen again, "originally Eve and Arlen Spencer."

"How could it have been in a trust for so long?"

"It is unusual, but not unheard of, for a trust to own a property for that long. It could be that Eve or Arlen's parents left the property in a trust for the benefit of their descendants. I'm speculating you understand. It must be into the second or probably third generation by now. Usually these things break up—too many heirs, somebody wants out. The property gets sold."

"Do you have the names of the trustees in your system?" I repeated.

"Nope. The contact is a law firm in Portland. Herrickson and Carroll. Hmm. Herrickson. That's interesting. Of course, old Frank was a neighbor of theirs, so he'd be a natural to ask to create a trust."

"I thought Herrickson and Carroll didn't exist anymore."

"Really? Frank is dead of course, but sometimes firms go on forever with dead partners' names on the door. The property tax bill must be sent some-where. Let me see." He clicked to a different screen. "Here it is. Herrickson and Carroll, care of Dunwitty, Moscone, Tyler and Saperstein, 185 Mid-dle Street, Portland, Maine."

I typed the firm name and address into my phone. "Thanks. Do you ever talk to the lawyers?"

"About this property? No reason to. No one's pulled a construction permit on it for as long as I've been here. As for the rest of the town offices, as long as the property taxes, town water and sewer, and so on are paid, we'd have no reason to reach out to them."

CHAPTER 21

I used my cell phone to call Dunwitty, Moscone, Tyler and Saperstein. A hyper-efficient receptionist informed me that all matters relating to the defunct firm of Herrickson and Carroll were handled by Mr. Tyler, who was currently in court. After putting me on hold for a few minutes, she returned to say Mr. Tyler could see me at eight thirty the next morning. Our meeting would have to be short as he was expected to be due back at the courthouse.

"Can I tell him what this is regarding so that he may be better prepared for your meeting?" She asked it in the same brusque tone that had characterized the entire conversation.

"The Spencer Family Trust," I answered.

"Fine," she said without a glimmer of recognition.

I said my hurried good-byes. Once again, I was in danger of missing the *Jacquie II*.

The boat was filled to capacity. Many visitors

had switched their tickets from yesterday's stormy
day to today's beautiful one. The group was full of
anticipatory energy, like they'd all been penned
indoors the day before. Children raced up and
down the boat while adults chased after them, and
the snack bar did a lively business.

On the ride out, with some difficulty, I found a
quiet corner on the lower deck to reflect on what
I'd learned during the morning.

If the black and white photo I'd found in Lou's
desk did indeed document a christening celebration, then there was a real possibility Frank Herrickson's goddaughter and her parents had lived
at Spencer Cottage. Which meant the beneficiary
of the Spencer Family Trust might be Elizabeth
Anderson.

Binder and Flynn couldn't dispute that Elizabeth Anderson was the single biggest winner from
the death of Bart Frick. Was she waiting in the
wings to claim her prize? I aimed to find out.

At the clambake, I played my usual hostess role.
One little boy asked me how lobsters mated and I
delighted in describing the lobster's complex life
cycle, as well as we know it. As I talked, he turned
his head, staring pointedly at his brother and sister
playing tag next to the bocce courts. I'd given him
way more information than he wanted.

At last, we loaded the lunch guests on the boat
and sat down to our meal. Livvie and her crew had
prepared a tasty combination of clams in a white
sauce served over baked potatoes, all of it rescued
from clambake leftovers. I loved this particular

dish, which Livvie had learned from our departed and dearly missed longtime cook. It was essentially the chowder we served every day, but in an upside-down, deconstructed sort of way. The meal was hearty and comforting, exactly when I needed comfort.

As I ate, I watched Page and Vanessa turn cart-wheels on the great lawn. They were both good athletes, keeping their legs straight as they flew into the air and landing gracefully on the other side. They shrieked as they played, working out their energy in a way we didn't allow when there were customers around. Emmy stood off to the side, holding Luther and watching her daughter. When Vanessa cartwheeled, her long tawny hair brushed across the grass. She was such a beautiful child.

It was painful to envision the horror that would come if she was Terry's child, and if she carried the long strand of DNA that doomed her to a loss of motor function and dementia. She was only ten. Maybe a cure would be found before she was old enough to experience symptoms. But what if it was a cure that worked only if administered before there *were* symptoms? In that case, denying Vanessa the knowledge about who her father was could de-prive her of critical information about her health. I began to see some sense in Chris's contradictory positions—not getting tested himself, but insisting Vanessa learn about her vulnerability to the dis-ease so she could make a conscious choice.

The second seating was as big as the first and

equally successful. The crowd was subdued when they boarded the boat for the trip back to Busman's Harbor.

Again, I sought out a quiet corner to be alone with my thoughts, but Mom sat down next to me.

"You haven't been in the clambake office for three days," she said.

"I won't be tomorrow, either. I'm headed to Portland first thing. Don't worry. I'll make sure we have steamers."

"Is this about Bart Frick?" She knew me too well.

"The Snugg sisters have asked me to help Ida."

She was quiet for a moment. "Then you should. Ida's a good person."

"She killed her husband."

"She did. But she also served her sentence and has led a good life since. I don't know what would have become of Lou without her. She certainly couldn't have lived out her life in Herrickson House as she wanted." Mom turned in her seat to face me. "If you don't believe in redemption, in the ability of human beings to change and lead better lives, then I don't know what you can believe in."

I squeezed her hand to show I understood. Bart Frick hadn't had a chance to become a better person. Someone had robbed him of that. But who?

When the *Jacquie II* pulled up to the town pier, Chris was waiting. I dashed ahead of the crowd and ran to him. He folded me in his strong arms.

"Why aren't you at work?" I asked.

"Night off."

"The cab?" Normally, during the season, Chris spent his nights off from Crowley's driving his cab.

"This is more important." He drew me to him again. "You are more important. I'm sorry. I've been a jerk about this whole thing. I see that now. I should have told you a long time ago."

"I know it's been hard for you, too."

He nodded. "It has. The whole subject ties me in knots. And I've lived with it over twenty years. I can't imagine how you feel."

The guests were off the *Jacquie II*. Our employees disembarked while Captain George and his crew buttoned the boat up for the night. As she walked up the pier, Mom caught my eye. She understood it wasn't a moment to intrude and went on ahead toward Main Street.

"I want to understand. And move forward," I told Chris.

He kissed me then, right there on the pier.

We walked toward our apartment, Chris with his arm around me.

"Julia!" As we passed the Snuggles Inn, the sound of Fee Snugg's voice came from deep within its porch. It wasn't unusual for her to be out there at that hour. Vee went to bed early because she cooked breakfast, but Fee stayed up until the last guests were in their rooms so she could lock up. Chris and I walked toward the porch so Fee wouldn't have to shout.

"Ida called. The police have asked her to come back to the station tomorrow," Fee told us. "They said they're re-interviewing everyone, but she doesn't believe them. Up to now she's been stoic, but tonight she sounded upset and scared. Have you made any progress?"

"Maybe. I've identified a suspect the police aren't looking at," I answered.

The deep worry lines in Fee's face relaxed. "Good."

"Please tell Ida to call Cuthie Cuthbertson and have him with her the next time she talks to the police."

Fee adjusted her thick glasses. "I will, Julia. Good luck. And hurry."

Chris chuckled as we resumed our walk home. "You've been busy. You'll have to fill me in."

But somehow, when we got to the studio, he didn't tell me his story and I didn't tell him mine. There wasn't much time for talking.

CHAPTER 22

First thing the next morning I took off for Portland. Maine's largest city was only an hour away from Busman's Harbor, though it seemed like a different world. Portland was a small city, to be sure, nothing like the Manhattan I'd left to return to Maine, but it had strong institutions, like museums and universities, and intimate neighborhoods, with shops, coffee houses, and bars. People went about on foot, connected to the sea and the cityscape.

And Portland had a rush hour. I noticed the pile up in front of me on Route 295 with just enough time to pump my brakes and join the throng. I found a garage not far from Dunwitty, Moscone, Tyler and Saperstein's offices and paid for parking for the first time in ages. Once I was on foot, I hunted along Middle Street for the building number. The clock was ticking. The receptionist had told me Mr. Tyler could only give me a few minutes and they were leaking away as I tried to find the building.

At last, I spotted the numbers, rushed through the glass front doors and jumped into one of the elevators, mashing the button marked 3.

The law firm looked like any other. Not floors and floors of lawyers like in New York, but a full, bustling office with cubicles in the center and offices ringing the outside.

The pretty brunette receptionist I'd spoken to the day before led me to Mr. Tyler's office immediately, practically cantering in her high heels so I had to fast walk to keep up. "He has to leave in ten minutes," she breathed. "Hurry up."

Mr. Tyler's office was traditionally decorated with mahogany furniture and glass-fronted barrister bookcases, a contrast to the sleek cube farm outside its door. The lawyer himself sat behind the desk, a tiny man who looked older than God. He extended a shaky, blue-veined hand. "Miss Snowden, I presume. I won't get up." He gestured to the leather chair opposite.

"What brings you all the way from Busman's Harbor on a lovely summer morning?" he asked. "If I were still fit enough to sail, at this time of year I'd be coming in your direction, not the other way around."

"I'm interested in a property that belongs to a trust your firm manages." It wasn't a lie. I *was* interested in the property, though not to buy.

He pulled back his thin lips revealing teeth such a startling white they had to be implants. "Spencer Cottage."

"What can you tell me about it?" I asked.

"As I'm sure you know or you wouldn't be here, the property belongs to the Spencer Family Trust. It has a longtime tenant. The cottage hasn't been updated in decades. I've been anticipating a buyer might turn up for some time, but I always thought it would be a developer. You're not one, are you? A developer?"

I shook my head. "What is the current status of the property? Do you know if the trustees or the beneficiaries have an interest in selling?"

"I do not." Mr. Tyler's wispy hair brushed his collar. "I haven't spoken to anyone connected with the property for years. The tenant pays rent, which goes into an account used to pay the property taxes, fees, yard work, and other necessities. The rental agency has someone open the house up in the spring when the tenant comes and shut it down in the fall right after she leaves. In the distant past, we might have sent any leftover money to the beneficiary of the trust. There hasn't been any such money for decades. The property, unimproved as it is, yields no profit, but with its view, and its waterfront, the value of the land is high. That's why I expected a developer."

"If you don't mind my asking, the property records at the town offices indicate the firm administering the trust is Herrickson and Carroll. How did it end up here?"

"I don't mind you asking in the least. I am the last living employee of Herrickson and Carroll. I worked there as an associate just out of law school. When Carroll died, Frank Herrickson soldiered on for another decade, but his heart wasn't in it. There wasn't enough business to keep an ambitious young lad such as myself happy. I signed up with Dunwitty and Moscone, as they were then. Not long after, Frank shut down for good and transferred his few remaining files to me. All of that business has been long since disposed of, except for the Spencer Family Trust."

"Have you ever met the beneficiary?"

"Mr. Tyler, it's time to go." A young man wearing a suit and carrying a heavy briefcase appeared in the doorway.

"On my way." Tyler rose unsteadily from behind his desk and made his way cautiously across the room to a coat rack. He plucked a straw summer hat from the top and turned back to me. "I met the original beneficiaries several times years ago. Lovely couple, the Spencers. But they'll be long dead by now. Their daughter has succeeded them. I haven't looked at the trust document in a long, long time."

The beneficiary was a woman. That was encouraging. "My interest is actually in the beneficiary. I believe she might have inherited an estate."

Mr. Tyler paused on his way out the door. The young lawyer waiting for him shifted nervously from one foot to another. "You don't say. What estate would that be?"

"Frank's estate. Can you tell me how I can contact her?"

He paused, his hand on the doorknob. "As I said, I haven't looked at anything related to the Spencer family in years. Mrs. Benjamin, our trust department paralegal, takes care of it. I'll introduce you on the way out."

Mrs. Benjamin turned out to be an imposing gray-haired woman with an air of ferocious competence. To my surprise, she stood up from her desk, went to a cabinet and took out a paper file. "One of the few left that's not in the computer," she explained.

She opened the file on the center of the desk and flipped through a few loose pages. "I've been taking care of this trust since the day I started, more than thirty years ago. As Mr. Tyler no doubt explained, the only asset remaining is the cottage. It no longer throws off any profit. Every year I send an accounting and a tax document to the remaining beneficiary."

"I'd like to know who that is," I said.

She nodded, still staring at the papers sitting on the open manila folder. "Back in the days when there was income, I sent the proceeds to an Eve and Arlen Spencer in Scarborough. Since they've passed on, I've carried on sending the documents to the same address. Let's see. Elizabeth Anderson, 29 Gorham Road, Scarborough."

As soon as I got out of the building, I glanced at my phone to see if I had time to drive the eight miles south to Scarborough and look around before heading north again to Busman's Harbor. I didn't. If I didn't go home now, I was going to miss the boat, literally.

I dialed Mom, who thank goodness picked up.

"I'm in Portland. There's some more work I want to do, but if I do it I'm going to miss the *Jacquie II*. I'm so sorry. I'll call Chris and see if he can bring me out as soon as I get to the harbor."

"Don't be ridiculous, Julia. We can manage without you. Everyone deserves a day off now and then."

"I had a day off, the day before yesterday, when it rained. I can make it back."

There was a long silence as I speed walked back to the garage where I'd left the Caprice. "Mom, are you there?"

"Julia, are you in Portland because you're helping Ida Fischer like you told me last night?"

I moved into the shelter of a hotel entrance. "I'm not sure. I'm in Portland because of Bart Frick's murder, but I'm not sure if anything I'm doing will actually help Mrs. Fischer. I'm convinced there's more to the story, and for the first time, I feel like I'm on to something."

"Then I'd much rather you finished what you're doing. It's more important. I'll close the gift shop during the meal and do the hosting. Everyone will pitch in. We'll be fine."

"I'll be on the dinner boat for sure." I felt lousy about no-showing, especially since I was supposed to be the boss. But when Mrs. Benjamin had said the beneficiary of the Spencer Trust was named, 'Elizabeth Anderson,' my heart had skipped a beat. I couldn't get so close and turn away, could I? "Okay, Mom. Thank you. Thank everyone for me."

A minute later the Caprice lumbered out onto Middle Street, the GPS on my phone set for 29 Gorham Road, Scarborough.

When I got off the highway and followed Route 1, my hopes rose and fell like a roller coaster. Parts of the road were residential and plenty of the homes looked more than thirty years old, like the Spencers could have lived there. But long stretches were commercial, lined by stores and mini-malls. Whenever I passed a run of those, my emotions plummeted. I was playing hooky, which put even more pressure on. What if I was wasting that precious gift of time?

When I pulled up to 29 Gorham Road, my worst fears were confirmed. There was a gleaming gas station and mini-mart with the number 29 over the door. I pulled into a parking space and sat for a moment, stymied. I decided I needed a bathroom and a coffee, so I pushed open my car's heavy door and headed into the store.

My business taken care of, I deflated again. The kid behind the counter looked sixteen at the max, unlikely to be helpful. Nevertheless, I tried.

"When was this place built?" I asked.

Blank look.

"Was there a house here before? Do you remember?"

Blank look.

"Is there anyone around who's maybe a little older?"

At that point, his brain engaged. "Earl. He's the owner."

"Where is Earl?"

"In the back." The kid pointed to a door beyond the restrooms.

"Thanks."

I found Earl at a cluttered table wedged into a corner of a tiny office, muttering over some paperwork. I knocked lightly on the door frame, and then louder, trying to get his attention.

When he did look up, he smiled. "How can I help you, young lady?"

"Sorry to bother you. The clerk sent me back here."

"Need to return something?"

"No, no. Nothing like that. I was wondering how long the mini-mart's been here and if there was a house here before it."

"You were, were you? And why were you wondering about that?"

"I'm trying to find the former owners. Or the daughter of the former owners. I'm not sure. It's all a little confusing."

He considered that for a moment. I wondered if he'd ask the obvious question: "Why?" But instead he said, "Then you've come to the right place. Come in, grab a stool."

I squeezed in through the door and sat on a dirty and very uncomfortable metal stool. It was in the opposite corner from Earl, but the room was so tiny our knees nearly touched.

"Yes, indeed there was a house here. I bought it when I built this place fifteen years ago. It was already business zoned. There was the house, a garage with a lift, and a couple of gas pumps. I knocked them all down to build this."

"Do you remember the name of the former owner?"

"'Course I do. Betty Anderson. She was going through a hard time, a divorce. She'd inherited the place from her parents and was happy to unload it."

Betty Anderson. Elizabeth Anderson. I was so close I could taste it. "You don't happen to know where Betty moved, do you?"

"After the divorce, she moved with her kid to a rental, but then she remarried. Last I heard she had a little house on Sunset Road. Her kid is grown. I heard Betty was widowed four or five years ago."

"Do you know her married name, the last name of her second husband?"

"Reynolds, I think."

"Thank you so much. You've been so helpful." He still hadn't asked me why I was looking for her. A Maine form of not sticking your nose where it didn't belong. "By the way, do you still get mail for her?" I asked.

"I don't think so, but I really wouldn't know. All the mail for the business goes to a PO box. Anything that comes here gets thrown in the bin."

CHAPTER 23

Armed with her current last name and the name of her street, I had no trouble finding Betty Reynolds's address using my phone. It turned out to be only a couple miles away.

The house was a cape, tidy but well worn, with a big glassed in sun porch on the front. The light blue paint on the house needed a scrape and a new coat. The shingles on the roof were cracked and jagged.

I got out of the Caprice and stood on the side of the road, thinking about how to approach. Shrieks and laughter came from the back of the house, the sounds of children at play. I crossed the street and followed the sounds.

A boy and a girl chased each other in the back-yard. They were towheaded blondes, the boy older, maybe eight, and the girl, about six. Both were in bathing suits and he held a hose, which explained the screaming.

He doused her and she ran, he gave chase until

he hit the limits of the hose. She ran back and forth beyond the water's reach. "Betcha can't get me! Betcha can't get me!" until neither of them could stand it any longer. Then she ran for the house as he ran after her.

"Can I help you?" The voice was cold, a protective mama bear. I would have responded the same way if a stranger had come into Mom's yard while Page and Vanessa played.

I shaded my eyes from the sun and looked up at the figure on the back deck. "I'm Julia Snowden. I'm looking for Betty Reynolds."

"You've found her. What can I do for you?" The woman was in her mid-fifties, with wavy gray hair, blunt cut above her shoulders. She wore a bright pink T-shirt with a pink-and-blue madras pocket the matched her madras shorts. She held herself stiffly, squinting at me with striking dark blue eyes. She wasn't happy to see me and I couldn't blame her, given the way I'd stumbled into her yard. "Do you own a property on Rosehill Road in Busman's Harbor?"

It wasn't what she'd expected me to say and it took her a few seconds to respond, but when she did there was no uncertainty in her answer. "I do not. I'm afraid you have the wrong person. Elizabeth Reynolds is a common name."

I didn't think I had the wrong person. The trail had been faint in places and broken in others, but it had led me to her door. The woman who hung over the deck was the right age to be the woman in the photograph. "It's called the Spencer Cottage. Is that name perhaps familiar to you?"

"Spencer is my maiden name. And we lived in Busman's Harbor when I was young, before I started school. But that was a long time ago. I'm not sure my parents even owned the house we lived in back then."

"If they were Eve and Arlen Spencer, they were the original beneficiaries of a trust that still owns the house. And now, I think, you may be the remaining beneficiary."

"Betcha can't get me! Betcha can't get me! Betcha can't get me!" The taunts were followed by shrieking, as before, but this time there was an "umph" and a thud, and then genuine crying. "Grammy! He pushed me." The girl came toward the deck cradling an elbow that was grass-stained and bleeding.

"I've told you kids a thousand times. Come in, I'll clean it up." She wrapped the girl in a towel, opened the screen door and turned to me. "You better come inside, too."

The girl, whose name was Samantha, was bandaged up and both kids were sent to put on dry clothes. Betty Reynolds returned from the bathroom and ushered me to a kitchen chair. The kitchen was clean and tidy, but the appliances were old, the cabinets painted wood, the floor and countertops linoleum. It was the comfortable home of someone caring and careful, who didn't have a lot of extra money.

She sat down, kitty-corner from me. "Let's begin again. I'm Elizabeth Spencer Anderson Reynolds. My friends call me Betty."

"I'm Julia Morrow Snowden. My friends call me Julia."

We shook hands, and then Betty rose and pulled a large glass pitcher out of the refrigerator. "Lemonade?"

"Yes, thank you."

"Now start at the beginning."

Starting at the beginning was exactly what I did not want to do. Because starting at the beginning meant telling her about Herrickson House, and Lou, Frank, Bart Frick, the murder, and the possible inheritance. It was one thing to tell her about Spencer Cottage. It was another to dangle a multi-million-dollar estate in front of someone who lived modestly, especially because I wasn't sure.

But nonetheless, throwing out caveats every other sentence, I stumbled through it. Betty Reynolds would have been an awful poker player. All of her emotions played across her features. Astonishment at the description of Herrickson House. Horror in response to the murder. Shock at the idea of an inheritance.

I had no doubt that she was hearing everything I told her for the first time. She hadn't killed Bart Frick in order to gain an inheritance. She hadn't known who he was or a thing about it.

"But I don't understand how you found me. Or how you knew to come looking in the first place." Our lemonade glasses sweated in the heat, leaving puddles on the glossy fake wood of the kitchen table.

I talked her through the chain of how I'd found

her, starting with the photo of Frank Herrickson I'd found in Lou's desk. At that point, she excused herself. She was gone long enough I worried she was phoning the police. She returned with a black and white photo in an inexpensive brass frame.

"Is this the one?"

"Yes! That's it. So you have a copy, too. Was Frank Herrickson your godfather?"

She sat down again. "Not that I ever knew. I found this in my mother's things when she passed. I kept it because it's the only photo I have of me when I was a toddler. I used to tease my parents that I must be adopted because there were no baby pictures of me." She took the image in both hands and studied it. "My granddaughter Samantha looked just like that."

"Does it say anything on the back?"

"Dunno." Betty moved the clasps, stiff with long disuse, and opened the back of the frame. The photo slid out, tan with age. There wasn't a mark on it.

"What do you know about your early life?" I asked.

"My mother told me we lived in Busman's Harbor when I was small. I don't honestly remember it. We moved to Scarborough before I started kindergarten. I've stayed in town right along. I married Bill Anderson when I was eighteen, right out of high school. It turned out to be a terrible mistake. I was directionless in school and I panicked about the future and married the first man who asked." She spread both hands out on the table. "But I did get my daughter Meredith from that marriage, so I can't regret everything about it. After I left my husband, Meredith and I moved back in with my parents. They were getting on. I'd been used to having older parents, but their declines came so suddenly. First my father, who died from heart disease when I was thirty. Then my mother five years later. I tried to keep up the house, but it was too much. I sold it to Earl Cabot to keep the bank from foreclosing."

"Grammy, it's too hot outside. Can we watch TV?"

Betty nodded without speaking. The kids had the answer they wanted and ran off before she could change her mind.

"A few years later, I met my second husband. Al Reynolds was everything Bill Anderson was not. He was kind, patient, a good provider. He treated me like a queen and Meredith was his little princess. Unfortunately, we didn't know it, but he had a bad ticker. He passed five years ago. Meredith is single again, too. She and the kids live with me." Betty looked up at me and smiled. "How am I going to tell her I'm an heiress?"

"*May* be an heiress," I emphasized.

"My parents were never ones to dwell on the past. 'The best day is today,' my father used to say. I was surprised and pleased to find this baby photo."

"Was there anything else in your parents' things that might help you establish your claim?"

"I couldn't keep much when we sold their house. I have a box of papers, that's all."

"Maybe look through it to see if there's a baptismal certificate with your godfather's name on it," I suggested.

"That's a good idea. Then what do you think I should do?"

"Dunwitty, Moscone, Tyler and Saperstein seems like the best place to start. You can let them tell you about the Spencer Family Trust and ask how to handle making yourself known to Lou Herrickson's attorney. If Bart Frick has heirs, they might also believe they inherit. And, the state police will want to talk to you, too."

She blinked. "I guess they would. You don't think they suspect me in this murder?"

"I don't think so. They can't prove you knew anything about it. But maybe check with your lawyer before you speak with them."

I thanked Betty for the lemonade and headed to the back door, the way I'd come in. Cartoon voices came from the television in the living room.

At the door, she said, "Can I give you a hug?"

"Of course." I hugged her back. "I hope the news I've brought turns out to be good for you."

"Me, too. But even if it isn't, you've still made my day. I'll tell this story for years."

CHAPTER 24

There were no cars in the driveway when I returned to Ida's sister's house. I knocked hard on the door, hoping Ida was home alone. When there was no answer, I knocked harder. "Ida! Are you here? I need to speak to you urgently."

"Julia?" The door opened a few inches. Ida's slightly bulging eyes were red, as was her nose.

I gave a slight push and Ida stepped back to let me in. "What's wrong?" I asked.

"You'll think I'm a foolish old woman, crying about the past, things that can't be changed." She led me through the living room into the sunlit kitchen.

"Is there anything I can do?" I cringed inwardly. I had come to have a serious talk with this woman, and to do that, I had to ask questions that would only cause more pain.

As if she sensed my discomfort, she looked at me sharply and asked, "Why are you here?"

"I have more questions and I'm afraid they won't help your mood."

"Will they help me stay out of jail?"

I was honest. "I don't know, but I think they will help us fill in some blanks and may keep someone else out of trouble."

She hesitated, but then gestured for me to sit down at the table and sat as well.

"Are you ready?" I asked.

"As I'll ever be. The past is not a happy place for me."

I cleared my throat. There was no delicate way forward. "You told me you went to prison for killing your husband. You didn't tell me you had a daughter."

"I don't like to think about her." Ida plucked a napkin from the holder at the center of the table. "I don't talk about what happened with my husband, if I can avoid it. I never talk about my baby."

She dabbed at her eyes with the napkin. I waited for her to be able to continue. "I married in haste, and repented in haste, too. I knew instantly it was wrong. My husband was cruel, both in words and deeds. He beat me on the second day of our honeymoon and he never stopped. Until I stopped him."

I reached across the table and put my hand on hers.

"I should have left. I knew I should have left, but I was pregnant, and then I had an infant, a toddler. I took on cleaning jobs. There were a few kind people who let me bring my daughter with me when I cleaned their houses. But without a car, I couldn't get enough jobs to earn enough to keep us.

"I should have returned to Busman's Harbor. I know that now. But I was too full of pride. Peg told me the first time she met Leland to stay away from him. I insisted he was a good man. But the signs were always there. I was too desperate to see them.

"On the night I killed my husband, he had beat me without mercy. He was always careful not to hit me in the face or arms, any place that would show. But that night, he lost control. I thought he would kill me. He'd returned from clamming, not a good day, which always set him off. He was in the garage, putting away his equipment when I came out and the fight started.

"Then, while he was hitting me, through the open window in her room, I heard my daughter cry out from her crib. He didn't seem to notice. He never heard her cry or picked her up. The louder she got, the stronger I got, until I was beating him. The louder she wailed, the more crazed I became. I picked his clam rake off the wall and swung it at him. He backed way, but not far enough. I caught him in the shoulder, above the collarbone. Blood spurted out of him, so much blood, and he went down.

"I ran to the kitchen and called for the police and the ambulance service. By the time I got back out to the garage, he was dead. When the police came, they took one look at me and sent me straight to the hospital. I yelled for them to get Frances. A policeman went into the house and carried her out. I never saw her again."

"Your baby's name was Frances?"

Ida nodded, unable to speak. She was crying in earnest by then. Great wracking sobs that were painful to hear. I couldn't think what to say. I squeezed her hand and waited.

"When they sentenced me to twenty years in prison, I signed the adoption papers. I didn't want her to grow up shunted from foster family to foster family. By the time I got out, she'd be an adult."

"But your sister—"

"Didn't know I'd had a baby. I was three months pregnant when I married. I didn't want my family to figure it out. My lawyer did mention Frances during the trial, and that was in the newspapers, but by then I'd given her up."

"On that particular day, what was it that set your husband off so badly?"

"I had a plan to leave him. I was sneaking things out of the house, a little at a time. Clothes for me and the baby. Cash. A few keepsakes. I kept them in an old crate in the garage. Leland found them that afternoon."

"And that's what made him so angry," I said.

"Yes. Mostly. But there was something he found in the crate that set him off more than anything else. A photo."

I already knew the answer. "A photo of Frank Herrickson."

She nodded.

"Frances' father."

She nodded again.

"Leland knew Frank was my baby's father." She paused. "Frank was a lovely man. Truly, I was in love with him, though I knew we had no future. Old Mrs. Herrickson was a harridan. When she found out I was expecting, and Frank was the father, she was furious. She was the one who found Leland Fischer and bribed him to marry me and move me away up the coast. He clammed out on Sea Glass Beach almost every day and often sold his whole lot to the Herricksons when they threw parties.

"I was embarrassed, ashamed, broke, without work. I thought Leland was my lifeline. Instead, he was the end of me."

"Were you angry Frank didn't stand up for you, didn't marry you himself?"

"I never expected him to. He was a lovely man, but not a strong one, and he never had the power to stand up to his mother. It was no surprise to me he didn't marry until after she was gone." She dabbed her eyes again and blew her nose. "Why are you asking about this? I thought you were trying to keep me out of jail. Everything I've told you only makes me look more guilty."

I took my time with my answer. This part of the conversation was delicate, and I didn't want to give her false information or hope. "Do you know what happened to your daughter?"

"No. I've tried to find out. But those were different times. Once I signed the papers, I had no right to know anything more."

"After you were charged, did you ask Frank for help?"

"I wrote to him at Herrickson House. I got a curt note back from Old Mrs. Herrickson saying he was out of the country. She said she was sorry to hear about my troubles, but she took no responsibility for them. She never asked about my child, her granddaughter."

"How did Frank react when you returned to Herrickson House?"

"At first, he was reluctant. I know he didn't want me there. I brought too many sad memories, too much guilt. But Lou found out I had worked at the house and was newly out of prison and demanded they hire me. Frank couldn't say no to her, any more than he could to his mother. I was desperate, so I took it. In time, we found our rhythm. I was happy to be back at Herrickson House."

"Did Lou know about the baby?" I asked.

Ida's brows drew together. "I never thought so. She never treated me as though she knew. I certainly never told her. And she had her reasons to keep her past in the past, too. All of us did."

I leaned across the table so I could look her in the eye. "I think it was Frank who arranged for your daughter's adoption."

"What?" Her big eyes blinked rapid fire.

I pulled the photo from my tote bag. "Is this your daughter?"

She took it from me, examining the photo through her tears. She held it to her chest, collapsing around it. "My Frances, my Frances, my Frances."

I waited again while she cried. "How did you get this?" she asked.

"From under the cubbies in Lou's desk. A woman named Betty Reynolds has the exact same photo. She lives in Scarborough. I think she was adopted when she was two by a couple named Spencer. Do you remember them?"

"Arlen Spencer was Mrs. Herrickson's driver. And Eve was the housekeeper," she answered.

"They were older parents. My guess is they couldn't have children of their own. Frank brought them baby Frances after you signed those papers. He set up a trust fund for their family. They lived for a time in the cottage across from Herrickson House, but then they moved to Scarborough. Mr. Spencer owned a gas station and garage there."

"They can't still be alive." Ida could barely get the words out. "Does this mean you've met . . ." She couldn't finish.

"I've met a lovely woman named Betty Reynolds. She has a daughter and two grandchildren."

"She's happy then?" There was so much tenderness, so much hope in Ida's voice.

I pictured the woman in the little cape house, tending to her granddaughter's scraped elbow. "She's had some ups and downs, like everyone. But yes, I think she's happy."

Ida opened her mouth to speak, but couldn't.

"She's the goddaughter," I added, in case Ida hadn't put it together. "She may be the one who inherits Herrickson House." When Ida still didn't speak, I continued. "I think Lou did know she was Frank's daughter, and in naming her the successor heir to Bart Frick, Lou did what Frank wanted—insured that Herrickson House went to a Herrickson."

Ida's sharp features scrunched together, working hard to comprehend what I'd said. It was an avalanche of information. "My Frances owns Herrickson House?"

"Maybe. And all of Lou's other assets, but not for sure. If Bart Frick has heirs, they may have a claim." Binder and Flynn hadn't turned up any heirs, but they hadn't found Betty Reynolds, either. "And then there's Lou's daughter. Lou definitively cut her out of the will, but you never know. With things such a mess, she may try to horn her way back in."

Ida nodded. She'd caught up to the tale.

"You lived with Lou all those years," I said. "You'd lost a daughter, and so had she."

"I had no choice," Ida protested. "Lou made a choice every month, year after year."

"How do you know that, since you never talked about the past?"

"Every month, a letter arrived from Florida, addressed in the same handwriting, with the same return address. Lou had me put them in her desk. She never opened a single one."

I flashed on the pile of envelopes I'd seen Bart Frick examining. Binder and Flynn had taken them. They must be close to finding Lou's daughter.

"So you see," Ida finished, "Lou turned her daughter away. I never stopped looking for mine." She dabbed at her eyes with a tissue. "You realize, Julia, grateful as I am for this news, you've made me look more guilty. The police will say I murdered Bart Frick to get a fortune for my daughter."

I didn't know what to say to that. I offered to stay with her until Peg came home, but Ida said she wanted the time alone. At the front door she asked, "What should I do now? Should I call her?"

"Give her some time," I counseled. "I've only just told her about Frank. Let her go to the law firm and confirm that connection. Then you'll know for sure."

"Betty Reynolds, you said. In Scarborough." Ida was already closing the door. She wouldn't be following my advice, I was certain.

CHAPTER 25

I checked my phone has soon as I got in the Caprice. I had enough time to drop in at the police station, tell Binder and Flynn what I'd discovered, and then catch the evening cruise of the *Jacquie II*.

But when I got there, the reception area was full. There were several clammers I recognized from the protest outside the beach access gate, including Will Orsolini. He sat on a bench with his wife Nikki and Duffy MacGillivray. I said hello to them, then checked in with the civilian receptionist. "The lieutenant and sergeant are in an interview. I'll let them know you're here when it ends. As you can see, there are several people ahead of you."

I sat with the clammers who waited with varying degrees of impatience. Legs jiggled, feet tapped, knuckles cracked. It was like being trapped the percussion section of a clown orchestra.

Will, Nikki, and Duffy, on the other hand, were relaxed, laughing and joking. Nikki, in particular, had lost the drawn, tense edginess from the last time I'd seen her. As I watched her, a gear in the back of my mind started to turn. Something about Nikki when we were kids, I thought. But the gear failed to catch on anything, failed to turn the larger wheel, no matter how hard I worked it. The memory never came into focus.

The door opened, and Binder and Flynn came out, along with Jamie and the lighthouse-loving Barnards. I'd been so bent on my mission I hadn't noticed their RV in the parking lot, but through the double glass front doors, I spotted it, in all its lighthousey glory.

Jamie walked them out.

"Ms. Snowden," Binder said.

"She wants to talk to you," the receptionist informed him, quite unnecessarily in my opinion. Why else would I be there?

"Interesting. We'll fit her in."

Outside, Jamie lingered with the Barnards. He shook both their hands in turn. This was the second time I'd seen him take time with them. Was he going to hug them? They were semi-adorable, at least when you got Anne in the right mood, but I was sure the police frowned on hugging witnesses, if that's what they were.

"Julia." Binder brought me back from my speculations. "I need to talk to Mr. Orsolini. Sergeant Flynn will speak to Mr. MacGillivray in the chief's office, and Officer Dawes will speak with Mrs. Orsolini. When one of us is done, we'll squeeze you in."

The waiting clammers, who were clearly there by police "request," booed and turned thumbs down on that. It didn't really matter if Binder jumped me in the line. I wasn't going to make it to the *Jacquie II*.

When Will and Duffy went off for their interviews, Nikki moved to sit next to me while she waited for Jamie. "I'm so relieved," she confided. "If Duffy hadn't come forward, Will could have had some real trouble." She sighed happily. "My mom's got the kids. After this we're going out to celebrate. We haven't been out since, I don't know when."

Jamie came back inside and took Nikki to the chair beside his desk. I waited with the rest of the clammers. Their fidgeting was contagious. I put a firm hand on my knee to keep my leg from jiggling.

Lieutenant Binder finished with Will first. He walked him out the door, shook hands and said, "Please let us know if you remember anything else. Anything at all."

"I will, for sure," Will responded. "I'll wait here for Nikki and Duffy."

Binder looked at me. "Julia, enter."

I sat in one of the guest chairs, but he didn't go around to the other side of the folding table. Instead, he stayed on my side and leaned against it, only a couple of feet away from me.

"I found Elizabeth Anderson!" I could barely contain myself.

"The missing heiress? How'd you manage that? Flynn's been looking for days."

I talked him through the chain, starting with Vera French at Spencer Cottage, to Oceanside Realty, to the Town Code Enforcement Office, to Dunwitty, Moscone, Tyler and Saperstein, to Earl's gas station and mini-mart, to Betty Reynolds. Flynn slipped into the room during my recitation, which only egged me on.

"You've already talked to Ms. Reynolds?" Binder scowled.

"Yes. I'm certain she's the Elizabeth Anderson mentioned in Lou Herrickson's will. And she's Frank Herrickson's daughter. When I told her, she showed me—"

"Wait! You *told* her?"

"Yes, and there's even more I didn't tell her because I wasn't sure." He frowned. "I admit, maybe I got carried away. But I haven't hurt your case. She didn't kill Bart Frick. She never knew about the will or the trust or Frank Herrickson. You should have seen the look on her face when I told her."

"And it didn't occur to you that *we* would want to see the look on her face when *we* told her?" Binder folded his arms across his chest.

"I'm sorry."

"I was able to follow most of the story," Flynn said. "But what I didn't hear, because I came in late, was why you thought to go to Ms. French's cottage in the first place. How'd you get on this path?"

Ah, there was the rub. I took a deep breath. "I got on the path, as you say, because I found a photo of Frank Herrickson and a little girl. In Lou's desk. When I was in Herrickson House." I said it very fast. I hadn't wanted to tell them, but there is no way to avoid it.

"I don't get it," Flynn persisted. "You found it when you were in Herrickson House the day Frick was murdered? Why didn't you tell us about this photo earlier?"

"No, when I was in Herrickson House yesterday."

"WHAT?" They shouted it at the same moment.

"What in world were you doing in that house?" Flynn demanded.

"Do you realize what you may have done to the evidence?" Binder was still shouting.

"I'm sorry." I never should have gone into that house. Which I'd known even as I was doing it. And yet I had.

"Okay. Tell us exactly what happened. Exactly what you did and where you went." Binder's face was slightly less red.

I took a deep breath and talked them through it, and in so doing threw Quentin and Wyatt under the bus as well.

Binder ran his hand over his smooth scalp. "We'll need to talk to Mr. Tupper and Ms. Jayne."

"I figured."

"You didn't go into the breakfast room?" Flynn confirmed.

"I stood in the doorway, but I didn't go in. You'll

have to ask the others. I don't think they did, but we weren't together the whole time."

"And you removed this stone that propped open the cellar door when you left?" He continued to press.

"But the door didn't lock behind me. It has to be locked with a key. I saw what I thought was the impression of a key in the earth where the rock had been moved, but the key isn't there now."

"Did you take anything besides the photo?" Binder asked. I shook my head. Flynn held his hand out. I slipped the framed photograph out of my tote and handed it to him.

"Did you notice anything else different from when you were there with Frick?" Binder asked. "Anything at all?"

"Besides in the breakfast room?"

"Yes."

"The pile of letters was missing from Lou's desk. I assumed you had taken them."

"Us?" Binder said. "Why would we have taken them?"

"Because I told you Bart Frick was looking at them when I first saw him."

Binder shook his head. "We didn't pick up any letters."

"Ida Fischer says the letters were from Lou's daughter. They might help you find her."

"Julia, we've got this case about wrapped up," Binder said. "Why don't you leave the rest to us? I believe you have a tourist attraction to run."

"Dining experience," I corrected, mumbling

under my breath. I walked out of the police station hanging my head. The day that had started with the triumphant discover of Betty Reynolds and her parentage had ended in complete disaster. I had really screwed up.

CHAPTER 26

Chris was asleep when I slipped out the next morning. He'd come home late. There had been no time to talk. I was determined to put the one last puzzle piece of Lou Herrickson's estate in place and then to be on the *Jacquie II* in time for work.

I drove the Caprice to Ida's sister's house, even though I could have walked. I had somewhere I wanted to go afterward.

Peg answered the door in a light-blue terry bathrobe, then called to Ida. When she arrived, she was in a pink polyester robe zipped up to her neck. "Julia? Peg said you wanted to ask me something more."

"The letters you told me about, the ones you thought were from Lou's daughter. Did they come every month, all year long?"

She shook her head. "It's funny you ask, because there were no letters in the summer, not in July, August, or September."

"Why did you think that was?" I asked her.

"I assumed because the daughter left Florida in the summer, as so many of them down there do."

"So there were letters in the summer, but not from Florida? Where did they come from?"

"No, no. There were no letters in the summer. At least not for years."

I thanked Ida for the information and turned to go. She called me back.

"I called my daughter," she said in a hoarse whisper, as if she was telling me a secret.

I laughed. "I knew you would. How did it go?"

"She was shocked. She'd had a shocking day all around. Her daughter was there and I mostly talked to her." Ida teared up. "My granddaughter. Mostly I talked to my granddaughter. We're all meeting up next week."

"That's wonderful, Ida. I'm so happy for you—and for Betty, too."

I gave her a hug, got back in the Caprice, and headed to Herrickson Point.

I parked up the hill opposite the gate to Herrickson House and looked down, over the boxwood hedge, toward the beach. I was relieved to see the chain link gate was still open and cars and pickups were parked in the lot. I'd worried my confession that Quentin, Wyatt, and I had been inside the house might have caused Binder and Flynn to demand the gate be closed again.

But they had not. Clammers worked along the

tide line. The Barnards' RV was parked up by the lighthouse.

I turned around, pushed through the gate to Spencer Cottage and entered its yard. Vera French was lying on the lounge chair on the open deck, in almost the same position in which I'd last seen her.

"Ms. French?" I called. "It's Julia Snowden."

She didn't move.

"Ms. French! Vera!"

Still no movement. I ran to the stairs, taking them two at a time and hustled across the deck. "Vera French!" Her skin glowed with suntan oil. Was she breathing? Was she a second murder victim? My heart pounding, I reached for her shoulder and shook.

"Eeeeek!" She sat up faster than I thought possible, knocking me backward as she did. As I doublestepped to regain my footing, she removed an ear bud from each ear. "You scared me to death!"

"I'm sorry." I felt the heat of an embarrassed flush creep up my throat. "I called from the path, but you didn't hear me." Even through the tiny speakers I could hear the music that had been pounding in her ears, more appropriate to aerobic exercise than lying in a deck chair.

"Well, now that you've got my heart beating, what did you want?" Vera demanded.

There were four chairs around a glass-topped dining table on the deck. I grabbed one of them, "Mind if I sit down?" I was in the seat before she could answer.

"Very well. Now, what is it?"

There was nothing to do but to go for it. "The morning Bart Frick was murdered, when I went in the house, he was in Lou's study, standing at her desk."

"What has this to do with me? Out with it."

"He was reading a letter from a pile of envelopes. Sealed envelopes. A very big pile."

Did she grow a little paler behind the deep tan? "I'm still waiting."

"I went back to the house the day before yesterday. The envelopes weren't there."

"What on earth were you doing in Herrickson House the day before yesterday?"

"Let's leave that for a moment. I was there. The envelopes were not."

She threw up her hands. "Then I suppose the police took them. Maybe they are germane to the murder."

"I thought that as well. So I asked them. They didn't."

Through her sunglass lenses I saw her eyes roll. "Very interesting tale, but I still don't understand what it has to do with me."

"You took them."

She pushed her sunglasses onto the top of her head. "Why on earth would you say that?"

"You took them because you wrote them. To your mother."

This time there was no mistaking. The color drained from her tanned face, leaving a thin ring of bright white skin around her lips. Would she deny it? Order me to leave?

She sunk back in the chaise. "How did you know?"

"I put bits and pieces together. You rent this house every summer, yet you said you'd never been in Herrickson House. Lou was a famous hostess and as neighborly as they come. Ida Fischer told me the letters stopped coming for three months every summer. You told me you were here for three months. There was one explanation that made all the pieces fit."

"I see. Did you tell the police what you figured out?"

"Not yet. They're not interested in the letters, but I think they'd like to know you were in the house the day Bart Frick was murdered, which you denied. And that you've been in the house at least once since then. If they knew all that, I'm sure they'd want to talk to Lou Herrickson's daughter. The woman who was cut out of Lou's will."

She stared at her lap, not looking at me. "Exactly what I was afraid of. That's why I took the letters. They all had my return address in Florida on them. I was afraid they would lead right to me, and combined with me being in the house at the time of the murder, I was afraid the police would jump to the wrong conclusion."

"You knew your mother had cut you out of her will."

"I assumed. She'd cut me out of her life."

I still couldn't get my head around it. Generous Lou, open and welcoming. "Why did she cut you out? It's so out of character."

"The short answer is, I deserved it. I know you all loved Lou, but she wasn't much of a mother. She spent her life pursuing men, falling in love with men, and then falling out of love again. I was a product of her first marriage, before she got smart enough not to have any more kids with any of the other husbands. I was a plaything to dress up when she felt like it, an inconvenience to be raised by maids and then sent away to school when she didn't.

"Despite the way she treated me, I was desperate for her love. If we couldn't be close like mother and daughter, I wanted us to be close like girl-friends, to get our nails done and play tennis to-gether.

"For a few years in my early twenties, I had that. We were both single, a coincidence of timing. My mother's habit of chasing and discarding men had made me the opposite. I was a clinger. I could never let go, never say die, no matter how awful the man was, or how clear he made it that I had to move on." She paused and lit a cigarette. "The most recent man had just pried my fingers loose when Mom divorced husband number four.

"So we had this period when we did everything together. We went to dinner, danced at discos. All the old flirts asked if she was my sister. I positively basked in her attention." Vera took a long pull on the cigarette and then pushed out the smoke. "You realize it's taken me years of therapy to be able to tell you this."

"You're doing great," I encouraged her.

"Right. Where was I? At last I had the mom I wanted and what happened? Frank Herrickson. We met him at the Bath and Tennis Club in Palm Beach, both of us on the same day. She started

missing agreed-upon activities. I'd show up at the
nail salon for our appointment. She never would.
She'd be gone overnight, then all weekend. It was
the nightmare of my childhood all over again. Finally, she told me they were engaged to be married.

"I stomped. I cried. I reminded her that she
hated being married. I listed every rotten thing
every husband had ever done to her. When none
of those things persuaded her, I lied." Vera took a
drag on the cigarette. "I told her she couldn't
marry Frank because I'd slept with him. 'I slept
with him first,' I said."

The breath whooshed out of my lungs. "What
did she do?"

"She slapped me across the face, accused me of
lying, which, of course, was accurate, and said she
never wanted to see me again." Vera stubbed out
the cigarette with more force than required. "At
first, I wasn't too worried. I thought she'd come
around. Even if she married Frank, I assumed it
would be for her usual two or three years. And
then she'd be back. I was the constant in her life.
Palm Beach was the constant in her life. And yet,
she left us both." Vera spread her hands in front of
her and examined her fingernails, which were
painted a glossy red. "I was sad, but I got on with
my life and waited for her return. When I married,
I invited her. I called and called the house in Palm
Beach. I'd always pictured us shopping for my
gown. She never returned my calls, never acknowledged the event was happening. My father was long
dead by then, so I had my own money. I walked

down the aisle alone, sobbing the whole way." She sighed. "That was the beginning of the end of that marriage."

"Lou didn't divorce Frank."

Vera looked at me. "How was I to know he was the love of her life? And that Maine would be, too. Their time in Florida got shorter every year and after Frank died, she never returned. So I took things into my own hands. I wrote to her every month. At first, the sole purpose of each letter was to beg her forgiveness. But later, my letters became like a diary, or a journal. I wrote about what I was doing, how I felt, my most intimate thoughts. I had no idea if she was reading them. I knew she never wrote back, but the letters weren't returned. I wasn't positive she hadn't read them until I saw them unopened in her desk."

"And eventually, writing letters wasn't enough," I pressed.

"It certainly wasn't working. So I found this house through a rental agent in town. She showed me lots of places, but I rejected them. 'Can't I get closer to Herrickson Point?' I kept saying. In the end, she showed me this place. It hadn't been rented in ages, had never been updated or improved. But the location couldn't have been more perfect."

"So you rented it."

"Every summer."

"Which is why you didn't send the letters in the summer."

Vera's hands shook as she lit another cigarette and inhaled deeply. I couldn't tell what she needed more, the nicotine or the time to gather herself. Probably both.

She continued. "Every Wednesday, as soon as the housekeeper—"

"Ida Fischer."

"Yes. As soon as Mrs. Fischer would leave for her afternoon off, I would go over and ring the bell at Herrickson House and wait on the porch for a half an hour. My mother must have known it was me. She must have seen me walking over from across the road. She never answered."

On the one hand, would Lou, with her old eyes, staring at the figure of a woman she hadn't seen in decades, have recognized her? Did a mother always recognize her child, no matter what? It seemed more likely that Lou, with her deep tentacles in the town, would have asked someone at Oceanside Realty the name of the woman who had rented across the road. Lou undoubtedly knew it was her daughter standing on her porch every Wednesday. I kept this thought to myself. "You never gave up."

Vera waved the hand holding the cigarette. "Not until the day my mother died." Her deep voice grew even deeper. "I always thought there'd be more time."

Lou had been a hundred and one. Vera was well into her seventies. How much more time could she have thought they had? But the picture of a senior citizen child, standing on her mother's porch, waiting for her to come to the door, to acknowledge her, to love her, made my throat tighten and my chest hurt.

I went into Spencer Cottage and found a glass,

filling it from the tap over the old soapstone sink and then went back out to the deck. "Here." I held out the glass. Vera took it.

After she'd taken a long, slow drink, I asked about the day of the murder. "You did get inside Herrickson House that day, didn't you?"

She put the glass down on the little table. "When I got there, the front door was closed. I knocked a few times and rang the bell, then when no one came, I tried the door. It was unlocked. I was certain Frick was inside. You'd just talked to him."

"Did you hear the murder? Did you see the killer?"

"Do you think I'd be alive, talking to you if I did?"

"I guess not." It was a miracle either one of us was still here.

"The house was quiet. Too quiet, I realized later. I went through the rooms, calling for Frick. I found him on the breakfast room floor. The place was a horrendous mess, things flung everywhere."

"I saw it."

She looked at me, surprised. "That day? He was dead on the floor and you didn't warn me?"

"No. When I was there again later. Not the body, the mess." She raised an eyebrow in speculation. "I'll tell you about it when you finish," I assured her.

"I knew immediately I was in terrible danger," she continued.

"From the killer?"

"That didn't even occur to me. The house felt so . . . empty. All I could think was the heir was dead, and I, the disinherited daughter, was in his house. I hightailed it out of there and didn't stop until I got back here."

"But you called 911." Her voice had sounded like a man's to the dispatcher.

"I couldn't leave him there for the housekeeper to find."

"She'd quit."

"So I understand, but I didn't know it at the time."

"And then later you told the police you hadn't been in the house."

"They seemed to believe me. I've never felt so relieved. But then I got to worrying about the letters." She lit another cigarette, her third since we'd been talking. "I didn't know if the letters still existed, but they had never been returned. I couldn't take the chance."

"How did you get back in? The police would have checked all the entries for signs of a break-in."

"They did. I tried them all, too. When I got to one of the cellar doors, I noticed a big stone next to the stoop. I moved it, on a chance, and sure enough, there was a key underneath it. I unlocked the door and entered a cellar room with a stairway. The door at the top was locked, but had a skeleton key in it. One turn and I was in the kitchen."

"You propped the outside door open with the stone. Your habit of leaving escape routes. Why did you leave it there?" I asked her.

"After I had the letters, well, the truth is, I've been going into Herrickson House every day. I haven't taken anything, don't worry. I've enjoyed spending time there, all the time I wasn't with my mother, seeing her things and trying to understand her life after she cut me out of it. The open door was my escape route if anyone ever showed up. I started leaving it like that."

"It's never the crime, it's the cover-up," I joked, and immediately regretted it when I saw the look on her face.

Vera snubbed out the cigarette in the crowded ashtray. "I didn't kill Bartholomew Frick. You have to believe me. I never wanted Herrickson House or my mother's money. All I wanted was my mother."

"I believe you. But you need to go to the state police," I told her. "Tell Lieutenant Binder and Sergeant Flynn your story. Get it over with."

She nodded, huddled in the chaise lounge. "I will."

"And give them back that key," I added, as I headed down the front steps.

CHAPTER 27

I exited the gate at Spencer Cottage into the glaring sunlight of Rosehill Road. Vera had given me a lot to think about.

If she was telling the truth, and I thought she was, Bart Frick had been murdered in the time between when I had left Herrickson House and she had arrived. How long could it have been? Five minutes for me to walk to the pedestrian gate, five minutes to chat with Vera, and five minutes for her to walk back. Maybe seven, because she was older and a smoker, but not long.

If Frick really was dead when she got there, it would have taken time for him to bleed out, even from a punctured artery. The conclusion was inescapable. The killer, or killers, had been in the house with me, as I'd feared. Frick had been attacked immediately after I left. I had been spared.

I hugged myself in spite of the warm sun. Now that I'd seen the room where Frick had died and understood the frenzy of the attack, I felt certain

the killer wasn't a discarded heir or a mistreated
housekeeper. It was someone who had been
thwarted, denied something they desperately
wanted or needed, someone who had planned the
act, since they were in the house, but who, once
there, had boiled over in a murderous rage.

The Barnards' RV was still parked by the lighthouse. I walked down Rosehill Road and through
the long beach parking lot to toward the big vehicle. Most of the clammers were packing up for the
day, but I recognized Will Orsolini down at the
tide line, hard at work.

The RV was empty, as I'd expected. After fruit-
lessly knocking at the door, I climbed the steps to
the base of the Herrickson Point Light.

Glen met me at the door. "Hullo, Julia. What
brings you here this fine morning?"

"I was about to ask you the same question."

Glen stepped back and raised his hands in
mock surprise. "I would think it would be obvious."

"It looks to me like you've broken into the lighthouse." I pointed toward the keeper's cottage
screen door and the formerly bolted wooden door
open behind it. "And the cottage. I'm amazed no
one has reported you to the police."

"The police have better things to do in your little town it seems, and the locals aren't anxious to
give them a reason to come back down to the
beach."

"Where's Anne?" I asked

He gestured toward the water. "Taking a walk on
the beach. She's always emotional once we com-

plete an area and check it off our list. Nobody's building new lighthouses. The number is finite and at some point, we'll be done."

He seemed down as well. I would have thought getting inside Herrickson Point Light would have made him feel triumphant. "You have some beautiful lights ahead of you, Portland Head, Nubble," I told him.

He nodded absently. As we talked, we walked toward the keeper's cottage. He opened the screen door and we went inside. An electric light hung from the center of the kitchen ceiling, but it was easy to imagine the keeper's wife and children, in the time before electricity, sitting at the central table, working on their schooling or fixing a meal. There were two light blue suitcases by the door along with a clear garbage bag containing sheets and towels. The Barnards had spent the night.

"Do you mind if I ask why you do it?" I said. "Why was it so important to stay in town until you could spend the night at this lighthouse? Why would you break the law to get in?"

"In fact, the door was unlocked when we got here, but you're right. We clearly understood we weren't to enter, much less sleep here." He shifted in his seat. "I told you before. The goal is to see them all."

"I understand. But why is that so important?"

Glen sat in a kitchen chair and gestured for me to do the same. "Our son was a policeman, in Tucson where we live. He was killed in the line of duty twelve years ago."

"I'm sorry."

"Thank you. We knew he had a dangerous job, but neither of us had imagined a world without him in it. He was our only child, twenty-seven when he died. Never got a chance to start a family of his own."

The Barnards' affection for Jamie and his attitude toward them suddenly made more sense.

"After Brian died, I was sad, but Anne was devastated. She felt she had no reason to go on. And then, one of our friends, hoping to cheer her up, gave her a snow globe with a lighthouse in it. Anne was fascinated by it. When she held it, it gave her peace. She became obsessed with finding the real lighthouse, the one the snow globe was modeled after. She looked at thousands of images online and couldn't find it. Finally, she said she wanted to find that lighthouse. She mapped out a trip to the lights nearest us, the ones along the southern coast of California. I didn't point out that none of them were likely to be the one. Why would you put a lighthouse from there in a snow globe? It never snows. I was so happy to see her planning something, desiring something, I didn't ask any questions.

"We went on that first trip. We traveled by car and stayed in motels. We were out of the house, we were learning new things, seeing beautiful sights. It was the first time either of us had experienced any emotion other than sadness since our son's death. When we got home, we immediately began planning the next trip.

"I know we're never going to find the lighthouse in the snow globe. Deep down, Anne knows it, too. But our lives go on. We have a reason to get up every morning. So if we get a little fanatical about our quest, so be it."

"You drove down to the beach the morning Frick was killed and stood at the chain link gate calling to him. Did you see anything? Hear anything at all?"

"We saw an older woman walk up on the porch and go inside."

"And while she was in there, no one ran out, maybe from the back of the house?"

He shook his head. "Not while we were there."

"Did you tell the police the whole story about the woman?"

"Twice. First to young Officer Dawes, and then to Lieutenant Binder and Sergeant Flynn."

So the police had known Vera was inside the house the day of the murder. I remembered how doubtful Lieutenant Binder had sounded when he'd told me her story. I'd put it down to normal police skepticism. She thought they'd believed her.

Glen leaned back in his chair and smiled. "I believe it was Officer Dawes who left the door here unlocked."

That would be like Jamie. The lighthouse and the keeper's cottage weren't crime scenes, and the story of parents who had lost a son would have touched him.

"Did you see the ghost of the Unknown Mermaid?" I asked.

"No, we didn't. But Anne keeps hoping that one of these days, at one of these lights, we will see a ghost. It would prove our son is still with us."

"He's still with you," I said.

Glen nodded. "That he is."

"Thank you for telling me." I stood up.

Glen stood as well, reaching out to shake my hand. "Thank you for listening. And for the tour of the harbor and your marvelous clambake. We'll never forget it."

"You're welcome. Come back if you wish, before you get too far down the coast. On the house."

"That's nice, but our plan is to keep moving. We've already spent more time in Busman's Harbor than we intended." He looked out the screen door. "Here comes Anne. We'll pack up our things and move on. Let's not speak of our conversation. She's still fragile and the murder here has set her back some."

"Of course not," I agreed. "I'll be going."

CHAPTER 28

As I walked back across the parking lot toward Rosehill Road, Will fell in step with me. He had a clam rake over his shoulder and a full bucket of steamers in his other hand.

"Hey, Julia."

"Hey, Will."

"Walk with me." I stayed with him as we walked toward his truck. "You were at the lighthouse talking with those Barnards? Interesting people." He said it casually, an observation, not an accusation.

"Yes, really interesting," I answered.

"Did they tell you why they're hanging around?"

Glen had, but I didn't feel like theirs was my story to tell. "I think they'll head out now that they've been inside the lighthouse and the keeper's cottage." I looked over at the RV as I said it. Anne and Glen were carrying their bags from the keeper's cottage, preparing to leave.

We reached Will's pickup. It was the only vehicle left in the lot aside from the RV. It was the quiet time when the clammers were gone and the swimmers and sunbathers hadn't yet arrived. He put his clam rake and pail in the bed of the truck.

"You went in to talk to the cops right after I did last night," Will said. "You're tight with them. Did they tell you anything?"

"I haven't been so much in the loop this time." I hadn't been in the loop with the police, but I had been busy. I'd found the missing heir and the missing daughter. I'd pursued the housekeeper and the lighthouse lovers. Everyone had told me their stories.

I believed Betty Reynolds hadn't known she would inherit Herrickson House, or that she had any connection to the Herricksons. She probably couldn't have found Herrickson Point on a map, and had no motive for murder.

Ida Fischer had loved Lou, of that I was sure. And was grateful to her for the second chance. I'd wondered why Lou hadn't told her she knew Ida had been her late husband's lover, the mother of his only child. But telling her that could also have given Ida the sense that Lou had hired her out of obligation, to pay the debt for what was done to her. That sense of obligation could have become a burden to both of them.

But not having told Ida she knew about her pregnancy meant Lou also couldn't tell her she'd found the daughter Ida had given away. Did Lou want to? Was she tempted? Ultimately, it had worked to both Ida and Betty's benefit that she hadn't—at least as far as this murder investigation was concerned—even if they hadn't benefited from knowing each other in life, at least so far.

Ida and Betty were out as Bart's killer.

I was surprised to realize how sure I was that Vera French hadn't murdered Bart Frick, either. At first, she'd seemed likely. She was incensed about the fence across the beach road and was always hanging around. And she could have been jealous of Bart Frick, even if she didn't stand to inherit if he died. To have her mother cut her out so easily had been unspeakably painful.

But Vera French hadn't seemed angry to me, she had seemed broken-hearted. She didn't want her mother's things. She had plenty of money and stuff. She had wanted a relationship.

I also didn't believe Anne and Glen Barnard had anything to do with the murder. At first, they had seemed so over the top angry about losing access to the lighthouse, I'd considered them. They had appeared to be so irrational. But the story Glen had told me explained their urgency—and it had the ring of truth.

I glanced into the bed of Will's truck. His clam rake lay there, metal shiny, tines perfectly aligned. It was not the rake he'd raised in the air when he'd led the mob at the gate. I was sure of it. He took a step toward me. I took a step back.

"Will, on the day Frick died, why was your truck parked at the end of Rosehill Road?" I asked him.

"I told you. I went after quahogs from my boat."

"But why would you park at the dead end? That's a terrible place to launch a boat." He shrugged, an elaborate display of nonchalance. I didn't buy it. "I didn't see you when I left Herrickson House that morning," I added.

"Like Duffy said, I was around the point."

My mind flashed on Nikki and his kids. They were adorable, a perfect family. They needed Will. No one had needed Bart Frick. No one mourned him.

I didn't want it to be Will. Everything in me re-belled against the idea. But that was an emotional response not a logical one.

The idea that had nagged at me at the police station the previous evening came suddenly into focus. "Didn't Duffy date Nikki's mom for a long time when she was young?" I asked.

"You're saying he's a liar?" Will growled.

"I'm saying he might lie if she asked him."

With an arching swoop of his arm, Will reached into the truck bed and grabbed the clam rake. I turned and fled as fast as I could.

Straight ahead lay the sand, then the water. If I went that way, I'd be trapped. I could run to the end of the parking lot and out onto Rosehill Road, but it was too far. Will was taller, stronger, and no doubt faster than I was. He would catch me for sure.

I could hear Will's footsteps on the sand-covered asphalt of the parking lot behind me. Despite the lead my jackrabbit head start had given me, he was gaining. I did the only thing I could think of, I headed straight toward the Barnards' RV, yelling at the top of my lungs.

As I got closer, I could see Anne was by the open

side door, still stowing their gear, but Glen was in the driver's seat. I shouted at him and waved my arms. He didn't look up. From that distance, I must have sounded like a noisy gull over the crashing waves.

I felt a whoosh of air behind me, then the clang of metal on asphalt, followed by a full-throated curse. Will had aimed the clam rake at me, but had missed probably by inches. He was closing in.

I ran for the RV. Glen looked up and saw me coming. He turned the key and stepped on the gas. Anne yelped and jumped out of the way.

Glen headed right for me. Could he cut Will off before he closed in? The pounding footsteps behind me said no. I dug in, propelling myself across the open space as fast as I could run.

"Whamp—whamp." Glen blasted the RV's horn. He was almost to us, almost on top of us.

"Move!" I heard Glen's voice through the glass of the windshield. The horn blasted again as I veered off around the side of the big vehicle and kept running. The RV thundered past. The noise and wind felt like I was standing beside a busy highway. I kept running, not daring to look back, trying to hear the swish-swish of footsteps in the sandy layer on the parking lot over the sound of my yammering heart. My calves were on fire and every step got harder, and slower. I could hear Anne yelling something off to my right, but I didn't understand and couldn't take time to look. The rocks the lighthouse stood on were thirty yards ahead. Soon I would come to the end of the point. I'd have nowhere to go.

From behind I heard a grunt. Pain seared through my shoulder. Will had hit me with the rake! I tripped, running an awkward three steps forward, but I was able to straighten up and continue. The rake clattered onto the pavement behind me again, too close, too close. Anne's screams changed from warning to terror.

And then there was whoosh of air and a horrible, sickening crunch of a noise, not metal on metal like a car accident, but metal on a sack of flesh, muscle and bone. Metal on a human.

The air brakes of the big vehicle groaned. I hadn't seen it, but Glen must have turned the RV around and, this time, instead of trying to cut Will off, he'd aimed straight for him.

Glen, Anne, and I all reached the place where Will lay at the same moment. He was on the ground, face up, bleeding from his forehead, his leg bent in a way nature never intended.

"He was going to kill you!" Glen yelled. He was red in the face, out of breath, shaking.

"He was, I saw!" Anne's tone left no room for doubt.

I shook all over, the kind of shivering that rattled my teeth and loosened my joints. "Is he—?"

Will groaned.

Anne pulled out her phone and punched in three digits. "I'm at the beach at Herrickson Point. We need an ambulance and the state police immediately. A man was hit by an RV. He needs to go to a hospital and he needs to be arrested. Yes, ma'am, I'll stay on the line."

*   *   *

Jamie and Officer Howland were the first ones on the scene.

"What happened?" Jamie signaled for the ambulance, which had arrived, siren blazing, at the entrance to the parking lot.

"He was chasing me." I was still shaking. "He hit me with his clam rake. Mr. Barnard over there," I gestured toward Glen, "saved my life."

I was afraid Jamie would ask, "saved you how?" but he was too busy with Will, who had passed out again. Maybe it was obvious.

A uniformed state cop who'd showed up asked the Barnards and me to stay around until the Major Crimes Unit arrived. I stood next to the Barnards while we waited. We didn't talk beyond the occasional, "You okay?" followed by head nods from the other two.

The ambulance was gone by the time Lieutenant Binder and Sergeant Flynn arrived. Jamie had ridden in back with the still unconscious Will, while Howland followed in their patrol car. One of the attendants had put a bandage on my shoulder where the rake had hit me. "A flesh wound," she said. "You're going to have a nice bruise from the force of the blow. When you're finished here you should go to the ER to get it properly cleaned and dressed."

"Did Mr. Barnard aim the RV directly at Mr. Orsolini?" Flynn asked, after I'd told him what had happened. Glen and Lieutenant Binder were huddled on the other side of the parking lot. Anne stood by the RV with the uniformed state policeman waiting her turn to be questioned.

"I don't know. Not on the first pass," I answered, "but the second was behind me. I didn't see any of it." I was glad I hadn't. Let Glen tell Binder what his intent was. "I believe Mr. Barnard saved my life." I touched the bandage peeking out from under my T-shirt for emphasis.

"What were you thinking, confronting a killer?" Flynn's posture relaxed a little. His question was more personal than professional.

"I didn't think I was doing that at first. But the more we talked, the more I realized it wasn't anyone else. Will was angry at Frick for cutting off access to the beach. He has a new clam rake, and he was here at the property that morning. He told me he used to give steamers to Lou, and what better way for a person in sand-covered rubber boots to get into the house than through a cellar door that took him to a staircase to the kitchen? He went into the house that way when he killed Frick and left that way, too. He waited in the cellar until Vera French and the Barnards took off, which is why no one saw him. Plus, I remembered Duffy MacGillivray was Nikki Orsolini's mom's boyfriend when we were little."

"So MacGillivray would have a reason to lie?"

"I think he would if Nikki asked him."

"Motive, means, and opportunity," Flynn said. "Orsolini was the obvious suspect from the start."

"He was," I agreed, "but I didn't want him to be. He has a wife and three little kids who need him. And he's always been good to me. Fair in business, friendly, polite. It's a shame."

"Don't waste your pity," Flynn said. "Plenty of people have their income threatened and don't kill the person responsible."

"You're right, I guess, but it still doesn't feel good. Can I go home now?"

"Yes. Come into the police station tomorrow to review and sign your statement."

"What will happen to Glen?"

"That depends on a lot of things. What he says. What the accident reconstruction team analysis shows about what happened here. The District Attorney's office will decide whether and how to charge him."

"I felt Will behind me. I heard the clang of the rake on the pavement inches from me right before Will was hit."

"I hear you."

"The Barnards' son was a policeman, killed on the job."

Flynn nodded. "He told us the first time we interviewed him."

There was shouting at the far other end of the parking lot. The state police had blocked the entrance. Behind their cruisers, I saw a familiar green pickup truck with landscaping equipment in the back. I couldn't hear what Chris was yelling from so far away, but he was insisting they let him in. I waved, using my good arm, to let him know I'd seen him and was okay.

Flynn looked over at Chris. "I'll let you go."

"Thank you. See you tomorrow."

I ran to Chris as fast as my aching legs could carry me.

CHAPTER 29

"Are you up to talking?" Chris asked. We were on the couch back at our apartment after a trip to the ER, where my wound had been cleaned and re-bandaged. I'd been given a tetanus shot, which was more painful than the scrape on my shoulder.

"I've been waiting," I said.

"I know you have. I'm sorry."

"Don't be sorry. Tell me."

He rose from the couch and began to pace like a restless runner before the start of a race. "My family isn't like yours."

He'd said it before, many times. I waited.

"My father is not Terry's father. He brought Terry up, but he never accepted him. There was always something missing in their relationship." He looked at me. I nodded for him to continue. "My dad is not a nice man. He drank, all my childhood, and when he drank he got nasty, biting, critical. For my sister, Cherie, and me, there was a sense that he did it out of love—in his own screwed up way, he wanted to turn us into better people. But with Terry, it was brutal, and constant, and not done with the slightest glimmer of love."

Chris stopped pacing and stood in front me, looking right at me. "My dad reserved the worst of it for my mother. He constantly belittled and be-rated her. If dinner wasn't on time, if there was a dish in the sink, if we were moping around the cabin. Anything could set him off."

He waited to see if I'd understood. I nodded and he went on. "One night when Terry was eigh-teen, Dad came home drunk. He raised his hand to Mom for the first time ever. Up to then it had been threats, rules, and insults shouted at the top of his lungs. He'd never hit her. Terry threw him out of the house physically. Left him sitting on the front step on his ass and slammed the door."

The pacing began again. As he walked, Chris clenched and unclenched his fists. Telling this was killing him. Not telling me, but revisiting it him-self, going into the dark cupboard in his head where he kept this stuff.

"My dad didn't come to the cabin after that. He was around town, living at my grandma's house. We'd see him from time to time. Cherie would go over to Grandma's to be with him. It meant more to her to see him than it did to Terry or me. She told us he'd quit drinking, but we didn't believe her.

"When he was twenty, Terry joined the Army. We hardly ever saw him after that. Then it was just the three of us, Mom, Cherie, and me. Grandma passed and Dad moved to Florida. We didn't even know where he was."

Chris sat down next to me and breathed in deep, as if he needed more oxygen to continue the story. "When I was a freshman in high school and Cherie was in seventh grade, Mom began to drop things. And forget things, and trip over nothing at all. She was adopted and had no idea what it was. We joked about how she was getting older, but she was only forty-two. She finally told a doctor about it. She was misdiagnosed, I think two or three times. Then came the terrible truth. But even then, she didn't tell anyone. Cherie and I didn't tell anyone. It was like we were ashamed."

I remembered the Chris I'd had the enormous crush on when he was in high school and I was in middle school in the same building. Wild man, captain of the football team, dating the head cheerleader, he hadn't seemed to have a care in the world. How wrong we can be about people when we only know their outsides.

"Then things got worse. Cherie told my father's sister, and she called Dad. He showed up like a knight in shining armor, saying he would take care of Mom. But there was a catch. He wanted to move her to Florida. I didn't trust him and I didn't see how Mom or Cherie could, either, after all he'd put us through. I was terrified we'd get stranded down there where we didn't know a soul, with a sick mom and a drunk or absent dad. I begged Mom not to go. He told her she had to choose. Him and his support or her kids and Maine."

Chris didn't say anything for a long time. I

could tell he was summoning the courage to tell the rest of the story. I waited, watching the sun sink in the sky through the big front window.

"Mom chose him." Chris's voice shook. "She chose him. I was furious at him, at her. Cherie was destroyed. I think she would have gone with them, but when he made it a choice between us and him, he pushed Cherie aside.

"The next day, Dad packed Mom up and drove her away. I was supposed to go to UNH that fall to play football, but I stayed home with Cherie while she finished school. She left town the day after her high school graduation and never looked back. I couldn't blame her.

"I didn't hear from my either of my parents for ten years. Then Dad called me to say they'd have to sell the cabin. It was time for my mom to go to a place where she'd have full-time care. I bought the cabin from them, as you know." Chris stopped talking. I took his hand. It was stiff with tension, but I didn't let go. "The sale was all done long distance. He never came up here.

"Since then, I've tried not to think about Mom, or Dad, or Terry or Cherie, but it's always there. Now that I'm grown, I understand my mother's choice a little better. She had to choose between living with two kids who really couldn't help her, and the grown man she'd spent a good bit of her life with. She probably thought she was doing Cherie and me a favor, removing the burden of her care. Her I forgive. Him I never will."

Chris was breathing heavily by the time he finished. The man I loved. He didn't cry. I'd never seen him cry. But I stopped fighting and gave in to my tears. It was worse than I'd imagined in all my fevered, fear-driven speculations. I hated the disease that had done this to him. I hated his father, too.

"And that's the story," he finished. "The long, sad story. You can see why I don't talk about it."

He put his head in his hands and I put my arms around him and we sat like that until long after the sun went down.

CHAPTER 30

It was the Monday of Labor Day weekend, the last weekday the clambake would be open to the public. We'd be open weekends until Columbus Day, but midweek only for bus tours that booked in advance. There had been a parade of good-byes every night for two weeks as our college students returned to school and our summer employees with teaching jobs out of town left.

I was fixing my plate for the family meal when I heard Mom's voice. "Julia, Wyatt and Quentin are here."

Mom stood across from me, flanked by the two of them. Bess stuck her retriever nose between them. I'd been so deep in thought, I'd missed Quentin's sleek sailboat gliding into our dock, them disembarking, greeting my mother, walking over to me. Who knew what else I had missed?

"Wyatt has preliminary drawings of Windsholme for us to see. Let's go down to the cottage."

"Livvie and Sonny can't come." Livvie would be back in the kitchen prepping for the next meal, while Sonny and his crew rebuilt the clambake fire.

"Wyatt can show them later." There was no mistaking my mother's anticipation. She bounced up and down on the balls of her feet.

"Sure." I put my plate back and followed them to the little cottage by the dock. Mom pushed open the door.

Inside, Wyatt spread a thin pile of large papers on the table in front of the big picture windows that looked out across the Atlantic Ocean to the horizon. We pulled up chairs and each of us sat.

"Before I show you these, I want to review your requirements." The skin over Wyatt's nose was creased, her voice solemn. I could tell unveiling her first set of drawings, however preliminary, was meant to be a solemn occasion. She cleared her throat, a delicate, hut-hum. "As we've discussed, the mansion is to be divided into three spaces. A public space, so the Snowden Family Clambake can expand its operations to include wedding receptions, reunions, corporate retreats, and the like. You've also expressed a desire for an apartment to be created on the second floor for Jacqueline to occupy during the summer, and a living space to be created from parts of the second and all of the third floor for Julia."

"That's right," Mom said.

"I don't see why I get the bigger—" I started.

Mom waved away my objection, as she had in

every previous conversation. "I'm at the point in my life where my need for space will only get smaller. You're the one who's likely to need more."

Wyatt looked from one of us to the other. Quentin kept his elbow on the table, his hand cupping his chin. They'd both heard the argument before.

When Wyatt was confident we'd run through the usual script, she went ahead. "I want to emphasize this is the first set of drawings we're looking at, based on my conversations with you and my assessment of the structure. I've also tried to take into account changes to the property that the feds, the state, and Busman's Harbor Code Enforcement are most likely to allow. You're on the water. You're on an island. There are a lot of rules." She paused. "Finally, though the budget is as yet undetermined, we all have a sense of what it might be. I've taken it into account as best I can at this early stage. As you know, building on an island triples the price of almost everything—infrastructure, transport of materials, equipment, and crew—"

"Yes, do show us," Mom interrupted. We'd heard all this before, many times, and would no doubt hear it many times again.

Wyatt turned over the first sheet of paper with a flourish. It was an elevation, the outside front of Windsholme. It looked, exactly the same. Only better. No plywood covered the big hole where the fire had burned through the roof. The cornices on the porch columns, missing as long as I could remember, had been replaced, along with the railing on the second-floor porch that jutted from the master bedroom. Wyatt's drawing fixed the steps, graded the land, and placed rich shrubs around the high foundation.

"It's beautiful," Mom said. "Show us more."

Wyatt flipped to the next sheet. The big old rooms on the main floor had been repurposed. The billiards room was a function room for meetings or ceremonies, the ladies withdrawing room was a dressing room, the living room offered space for receptions. The great hall was for dancing. The dining room and window-walled breakfast room were set up with many tables for sit-down meals, so we could book parties and not worry so much about the weather. Restrooms and closets had been placed in spaces that had previously been pantries and passages for servants.

Mom pointed to the kitchen. "It's on the main floor?"

"Caterers aren't going to want to run up and downstairs," Wyatt answered.

I expected Mom to flinch. The china cabinets and linen closets on the balcony that ringed the two-story kitchen were still intact, and though she'd never lived in Windsholme, I thought it would be hard for her to let them go.

But she didn't so much as bat an eyelid. "And this?" she asked, pointing again.

"The back stairway repositioned for private access to your residence. Do you want to see it?"

"Yes, yes!" Mom clapped her hands.

Wyatt had done a good job with the living space,

too. Mom's apartment made efficient use of one half of the second floor. It included a small kitchen, large sitting room, bedroom, and bath.

Mom asked a lot of detailed questions. Could the bedroom hold a queen-size bed? Could a desk fit here? An eating table there? She pointed at the spaces on the drawing with her long, beautiful fingers as she asked. She'd already moved in mentally.

I couldn't get there. Wyatt had made great use of the other half of the second floor, and all of the third. As she showed me my space, I tried to imagine the view of the Atlantic from my office, the straight line of the horizon. But my father's old office in Mom's house in town kept pushing the new one out of the frame.

I looked around the crowded cottage. It had only two bedrooms. Livvie's family would outgrow it. Had already outgrown it. Maybe they'd use the new space at Windsholme and I'd settle here.

Maybe my own family would need the second bedroom someday.

Chris coming clean about his family history had been like a fog lifting. Since the day he'd told me, he'd been noticeably happier, smiling more, laughing more, an extra spring in his step. I'd been happier, too. I no longer felt like I was tiptoeing across a minefield.

He'd agreed not to approach Emmy about the DNA test or anything equally scary. "My family was so blindsided when my mother got sick. I wanted to spare them. I can see I went about it the wrong way." He had been back to visit his brother in prison and he believed Terry might be willing to talk to Emmy after he got out.

Wyatt was still talking, walking us through the rest of the drawings. Quentin asked some technical questions and occasionally asked Wyatt why she'd chosen to do this or that. The design would need refinement, but overall I had to admit, it was darn near perfect.

"I'm so glad you all like it." Wyatt beamed at the three of us. "We have a long way to go, a lot of detail and decisions, a lot of logistics and legalities, but this is a good start."

"Wyatt's going to have more than your project to bring her to town," Quentin said.

"Really?" Mom raised an eyebrow. Wyatt's ex-fiancé was still in the harbor, but he and his yacht were expected to leave for warmer climates soon, as would Quentin.

"I'm doing a project on Rosehill Road," Wyatt said.

"Not Herrickson House!" It came out louder than I intended.

It had become clear Betty Reynolds would inherit the estate, but changing the mansion was the last thing Lou would have wanted.

"No," Wyatt said. "Not Herrickson House. Spencer Cottage. Betty Reynolds and her family plan to move into Herrickson House as soon as they're allowed. Ida Fischer is going to live there, too, back in her old rooms. The Spencer Family Trust is selling the cottage to pay the taxes on the rest of the estate. Vera French is buying it. We're remodeling top to bottom." Wyatt was clearly pleased.

"That's wonderful," Mom said.

"And, Betty's selling the beach and the parking lot to the town for a dollar," Quentin added. "It's all arranged."

I doubted it was. There were bound to be plenty of contentious Town Meetings about the cost of keeping up the parking lot and the potential liability caused by the unguarded ocean. But it would work out in the end. The beach was too important to the town.

My mother put her arm around me and squeezed. "Lou would have been so happy."

From outside the windows the *Jacquie II's* whistle sounded. Our dinner guests were arriving in minutes. It was time to get back to work.

RECIPES

Livvie's Linguini with Clam Sauce

In Steamed Open, *Livvie makes the linguini with clam sauce for the family meal—the meal the employees eat between lunch and dinner service. In reality, it is a recipe from my husband's Italian family, served at their Christmas Eve Feast of Seven Fishes every year.*

Ingredients

4 6.5-ounce cans chopped clams
¼ cup plus 1 Tablespoon olive oil
4 anchovies from a tin, chopped
2 large cloves garlic, minced, divided
⅛ teaspoon red pepper flakes (optional)
¼ cup finely chopped fresh Italian (flat leaf) parsley, divided
1 cup panko style bread crumbs
1 package (16 oz.) linguini
salt & pepper to taste

Instructions

Mix half the garlic and half the parsley with the breadcrumbs. Stir in 1 T of olive oil. Toast in a small frying pan until lightly browned. Set aside.

Prepare the linguini in boiling salted water. Cook for 7 minutes before draining. The linguini will still be undercooked. Don't worry, it will finish cooking in the sauce.

Gently heat the remaining olive oil over medium heat. Add the anchovies and red pepper flakes, if using, and stir until anchovies have nearly melted.

Add the remaining garlic and cook for two minutes longer, being careful to not burn the garlic. Add the cans of clams including their broth. Increase heat and bring to a boil.

Add the cooked pasta. Lower heat and cook until pasta is al dente. Stir in the parsley. Add salt and pepper, if desired.

Serve pasta and pass the breadcrumbs to sprinkle on top.

Serves 4-6

Peg's Famous Clam Dip

Ida Fischer's sister Peg may claim credit for this dip recipe in the book, but this is my husband Bill Carito's famous clam dip, his most requested dish whenever we ask hosts, "What can we bring?"

Ingredients

4 6.5-ounce cans minced clams, drained, reserving liquid
1 clove garlic
2 8-ounce packages cream cheese
2 Tablespoons chopped chives
2 teaspoons Worcestershire Sauce
1 Tablespoon lemon juice
2 Tablespoons reserved clam liquid, plus more as desired
½ teaspoon salt

Instructions

Start food processor and drop garlic clove through tube. Process until finely chopped.

Remove processor cover and add cream cheese, chives, Worcestershire sauce, lemon juice, clam liquid, and salt. Process 10-20 seconds until well combined. Turn out into a bowl.

Fold in clams and refrigerate for at least two hours.

Just before serving, remove from refrigerator and stir, adding more clam juice, if necessary, to desired consistency.

Serve with potato chips and/or corn chips.

Clam Potato Casserole

Julia characterized this hearty comfort meal as a "deconstructed clam chowder," and it is. At the Snowden Family Clambake this meal can be made entirely from clambake ingredients, but in this version, we've adapted it for home use.

Ingredients

4 potatoes, baked
3 6.5-ounce cans minced clams, drained, with
   ¼ cup liquid reserved
4 ounces butter, melted
4 ounces heavy cream
4 ounces thick cut bacon, chopped and cooked
   until crisp
1 bunch scallions, trimmed and thinly sliced
1 cup shredded cheddar cheese
⅛ cup snipped chives for garnish

Instructions

Preheat oven to 350 degrees F.

Peel the potatoes and cut into ¼ inch cubes. Put in bowl. Stir in clams, reserved clam liquid, butter, cream, bacon, and scallions.

Turn out into 2-quart casserole dish.

Top with shredded cheese.

Bake for 20-25 minutes, until cheese is melted.

Top with chives.

Serves 6

Ma's Sour Cream Coffee Cake

This recipe is from a book of handwritten cards given to me by my grandmother the Christmas before she died. It is delicious and smells wonderful as it bakes.

Ingredients

For the cake
2 cups flour
1 teaspoon baking soda
1 teaspoon baking powder
1 stick of butter, softened (1 quarter pound)
1 cup sugar
2 eggs
½ pint sour cream

For the "topping"
1 cup chopped walnuts
1 teaspoon cinnamon
2 Tablespoons brown sugar

Instructions

Preheat oven to 375 degrees F.

Using a mixer, mix the ingredients for the cake until smooth and integrated.

Using your fingers, mix the "topping" ingredients.

Pour one half of the cake mixture into a greased

tube pan. Sprinkle one half of the "topping" over it. Pour in the rest of the cake mixture. Sprinkle the rest of the "topping" over the top.

Bake for 35 minutes.

ACKNOWLEDGMENTS

Several of the previous Maine Clambake Mysteries have looked at the star of the clambake show—the Maine lobster. That is especially true of the third book, *Musseled Out,* which is about the lobstering life. But what about the clam, who gives the bake its name? The clam appears in two of the dishes served at the Snowden Family Clambake. The quahog, or hard shell clam is featured in the chowder that is served as the first course. This book focuses on the soft shells, called "steamers," which are cooked in the shell along with the lobsters and served as a part of the main course.

Clamming for soft shells can be a fun and rewarding pastime on a vacation day, or it can be a backbreaking commercial labor. Either way, in Maine, it is done by hand, with tools that have been used for over a century. For those who want to try it firsthand, clamming is free at several Maine state beaches. You can only take a peck, but that shouldn't be a problem.

For clam facts, I relied on *The Compleat Clammer*, by Christopher R. Reaske (Burford Books), which is about clamming on Shelter Island, New York, but is quite widely applicable.

For the ins and outs of oceanfront property

ownership in Maine, I consulted *Public Shoreline Access in Maine: A Citizens Guide to Ocean and Coastal Law,* third edition, produced by the Maine Sea Grant College Program, Maine Coastal Program/Department of Agriculture, Conservation and Forestry, and Wells National Estuarine Research Reserve. The history of the Maine shoreline is complicated and much litigated, so I appreciated this straightforward publication.

For those who have lived in or visited the Boothbay Harbor region, the story of the ghost of Herrickson Point Light will seem "eerily" familiar. For my research, I consulted *Ghosts of the Boothbay Region* by Greg Latimer (Haunted America). Of course, I changed the story to fit my characters and my timeline, and added some embellishments of my own.

Fellow Maine mystery author Brenda Buchanan provided enough baseline information to get me going on the inheritance part of the plot. The folks in the Registry of Probate in Wiscasset, Maine, were enormously helpful. All mistakes, intended and inadvertent, are my own.

Emily Gozzi's mom won naming rights at a charity auction and Emily provided the name "Willis Orsolini." I'm not sure what you expected, Emily, but I hope I did you proud.

My great and good friend Jon Anton suggested the title *Steamed Open.* He passed away as I finished the manuscript, so he never got to see it in print, but I will always be grateful and will never forget.

I'd like to thank the Wicked Cozy Authors, to whom this book is dedicated. We've blogged together for five years, but our mutual support society has been so much more than that. I honestly don't believe I could have done it without you, Jessie Crockett (Jessica Ellicott), Sherry Harris, J.A. Hennrikus (Julia Henry), Edith Maxwell (Maddie Day), and Liz Mugavero (Cate Conte). (All my friends are like drag queens—they all have two names.) An extra special shout out to Sherry Harris, who reviewed this manuscript while meeting the exact same deadline for the seventh book in her Sarah Winston Garage Sale Mysteries.

I'd like to also acknowledge my fellow Maine Crime Writers who have been so supportive of me, especially now that I've moved to Maine full-time.

Thank you to my editor at Kensington, John Scognamiglio, also Karen Auerbach, Robin Cook and the folks in production, and Ben Perini, who has done the wonderful Maine Clambake covers. Thank you also to my agent, the fabulous John Talbot.

Finally, to my family, who put up with me writing blogs throughout the holidays to support the publication of *Stowed Away*, missing my granddaughter's birthday three years in a row to attend an annual conference, being in "book jail" and useless for any work or fun around the house, and generally dragging them to book events, conferences, and on research trips. Special thanks to my husband, Bill, for the clam recipes. Thank you, Bill Carito; Robert, Sunny, and Viola Carito; and Kate and Luke Donius. You all make it possible to do what I do.